The woman with the
gun was beautiful

She was also scared. Mark Stewa... ...ee the shadow of fear in her eyes. After thi... ...ng a cop, he was good at reading s...

"So you've come... ...getting a gun."

"That's the g...

"And now you'... ...thoughts?" he asked.

She gave him an u... ...ble glance. "I came here to learn to shoot. And that's what I intend to do. Tell me, Mr. Stewart, do you grill all your paying customers this way?"

He tried a smile on her. "Actually, I haven't come to the grilling part yet."

When she didn't smile back, he continued. "I can tell you're in some kind of fix, Ms. Myers. Believe it or not, that's the worst time to think about getting a gun. Scared people don't always make the best decisions about firearms."

"It really isn't any of your business, is it?"

He could tell her he was a cop, but some instinct warned him not to. "It wouldn't hurt to talk about whatever's bothering you," he said instead.

She moved to the front of the desk, and he thought she was going to confide in him, after all.

Just before she turned and walked out the door.

Dear Reader,

My father taught me a lot about life—and about men. When I was old enough to shoot a basketball, Dad taught me never to back down to the boys on the court. When I was old enough to get better report cards than my brothers, Dad taught me that standing out meant standing up for myself. As I grew to womanhood, Dad encouraged me never to date anyone who didn't champion my dreams. And when I fell in love with a wonderful man, Dad had only two words to say: Marry him. Best advice he ever gave me.

As perhaps you can see, the father-daughter relationship is a very special one to me. That's why fathers and daughters are such an important part of *Her Protector.* Robyn Myers adores her dad. However, he has secrets that are destroying the family, and Robyn's love for him is tested as never before. Mark Stewart has father-daughter problems of a different kind. He wants to make up to his daughters for all his past mistakes—which it seems they will never forgive.

I hope you enjoy following the adventures of Mark and Robyn as they discover not only romantic love, but all the bittersweet ups and downs between fathers and daughters.

Ellen James

Books by Ellen James

HARLEQUIN SUPERROMANCE

Don't miss any of our special offers. Write to us at the following address for information on our newest releases.

Harlequin Reader Service
U.S.: 3010 Walden Ave., P.O. Box 1325, Buffalo, NY 14269
Canadian: P.O. Box 609, Fort Erie, Ont. L2A 5X3

HER PROTECTOR
Ellen James

Harlequin Books

TORONTO • NEW YORK • LONDON
AMSTERDAM • PARIS • SYDNEY • HAMBURG
STOCKHOLM • ATHENS • TOKYO • MILAN
MADRID • WARSAW • BUDAPEST • AUCKLAND

For my dad—we miss ya, Jake

ISBN 0-373-70781-9

HER PROTECTOR

HER PROTECTOR

CHAPTER ONE

THE WOMAN WITH the gun was beautiful. She was also scared, and doing her damnedest not to show it.

Mark studied her. She had russet hair cut short, but not too short—a few stray tendrils had been left to curl against her cheeks and at the back of her neck. Her eyes were a clear hazel, but Mark could see a shadow of fear in them. He also saw just a hint of desperation. He was good at reading subtle little signs like that. After thirteen years of being a cop, he was very good at reading people.

He was the one who'd placed the gun in her hand a few moments ago. Now she gazed down at it, her expression changed to one of mingled disgust and determination.

"Second thoughts?" Mark asked casually.

She gave him an unreadable glance. "I came here to learn how to shoot. And that's just what I intend to do."

He wondered why she needed a gun. What was she afraid of? As a police detective, he'd often seen the results of fear, the things people could do when they were pushed to the brink. He shook his head. Not his problem. At this particular point in time he wasn't a police detective—not officially, anyway. He was on leave from the department, whether he liked it or not. To keep from going stir-crazy he'd signed on here at the local shooting range, and that meant he was currently an instructor in the fine art of using firearms. So why wasn't he instructing?

"Maybe that's not the right type of weapon for you," he told the woman. "Maybe you'd like to try out something a little...smaller."

She frowned at the Beretta automatic in her hand. "It'll get the job done, won't it?"

"Depends on the job," he remarked.

An oddly bleak expression flickered across her face. "I've never held a gun before now," she said in a low voice. "But if it's to keep a promise—" She broke off abruptly. He could see the obvious effort she made to conceal all emotion behind rigid features. "Anyway, I just want to find out if I can handle this thing. *Can* we get on with it?"

Mark positioned her at a lane, and began setting the target: the standard outline of a human figure. Then, after a second's thought, he changed the target to a plain old bull's-eye. It seemed more benign somehow. Not that there could ever be anything benign about shooting a gun. He became aware of the ache in his leg, a reminder of the bullet that not too long ago had just about sheared his femur...the bullet, in fact, responsible for his enforced absence from the police force. No, there was nothing benign about guns.

He waited until the woman had the sound dampeners over her ears. Only then did he load the gun for her, sliding the clip into place.

"Now," he said, "use your left hand as a support. Arms fully extended...that's good. No, don't squint. You're not going to pull the trigger. Just squeeze it..."

She held the gun for so long it seemed she'd changed her mind, after all. She didn't say a word, didn't move, and an uneasy waiting filled the air.

Then, without giving any warning, she fired. The shot went wide.

"Try to visualize where the bullet will hit," Mark told her. "It's not enough to look down the sight. Shooting is a mental exercise, as much as anything else. You're squinting again...that's better."

After an initial shakiness, she settled in. She focused closely on his instructions, a resolute calm seeming to take her over. One shot, then another and another. She was an able student, and she possessed a natural skill at the endeavor.

Mark stepped back to let her try it on her own. She seemed to have forgotten his presence, all her concentration focused now on that bull's-eye. Robyn Myers, that was how she'd introduced herself when she'd first walked in here. Once again he wondered what had made Robyn Myers pick up a gun for the first time in her life. He noted the tense line of her shoulders, the effort she put into holding her arms absolutely steady. In the short time she'd been practicing, her aim was improving rapidly. A natural, all right.

At last Mark brought the target forward, the bull's-eye swaying back and forth as it drew closer. "Not bad," he said, observing the smattering of bullet holes.

She set down the gun and pushed off the ear protectors. "I think I'd like to get out of here," she said, her voice brittle. Without waiting for his response, she hurried through the door and toward the front reception area.

Mark caught up to her. "Have a seat in the office," he said. "I'd like to talk to you for a few minutes."

She gave him a skeptical glance. "The lesson's over, isn't it? I got a passing grade, didn't I?"

"Yes on both counts. But I still think we should talk." He ushered her into the office and pulled up a chair so she could sit in front of the cluttered desk. He sat down behind it, grimacing a little as the pain flared in his leg.

"What's wrong?" she asked.

"Let's just say I'm recovering from an on-the-job injury." He debated how to start; something told him that Robyn Myers wouldn't take kindly to what he wanted to say. Meanwhile, she leaned forward and picked up the photograph displayed at one side of the desk.

"Nice family," she said. The photo showed a smiling brunette and two young boys.

"Afraid I can't take any credit," he said. "That's Benjamin's family." At her inquiring look, he added, "Benjamin's the one who owns this place. He's a friend of mine from way back."

"I see. And he doesn't mind you appropriating his office." Her tone was sardonic.

"Just as long as I don't make a habit of it." He gazed for a few seconds more at the photograph. "My own kids are pretty much grown up," he was surprised to hear himself saying. Robyn Myers gave him a considering look this time, and he figured he was getting offtrack.

"Ms. Myers," he said, "for somebody who'd never shot a gun before, you did good back there. Surprisingly good."

She shrugged wearily. "It's not something I want to be good at. Before yesterday, it's not something I'd even have considered."

He let a pause settle between them, and then he spoke. "What happened yesterday?"

Immediately she was on her guard again. "Nothing that concerns you, Mr. Stewart."

Maybe she was right. Then again, being a cop meant you poked your nose into other people's troubles. And Robyn Myers was in trouble...he didn't have any doubts about that much.

"So," he said. "You came in here today because you're thinking about getting a gun."

"That's the general idea. Tell me, Mr. Stewart, do you grill all paying customers this way?"

He tried a smile on her. "Actually, I hadn't come to the grilling part yet."

She didn't smile back. "What's your point, Mr. Stewart?"

"I can tell you're in some kind of fix, Ms. Myers," he said. "Believe it or not, that's probably the worst time to think about getting a gun. You're scared. And scared people don't always make the best decisions about things like firearms."

She stood, her cheeks turning a slightly indignant pink. "It really *isn't* any of your business, is it, Mr. Stewart?"

He could tell her he was a cop, but some instinct warned him not to. "It wouldn't hurt to talk about it," he said. "Whatever it is that's bothering you."

It was there again in her eyes, the shadow of fear.

She stood in front of the desk, and he thought she was going to confide in him, after all. But then she withdrew behind that rigid mask, just before she turned and walked out the door.

"HOW IS HE, Mom?"

"He's sleeping at last," Nina Myers said anxiously. "That's a good thing, the doctors say. But how can anything be good right now? You go sit with him for a bit, Robyn. If he wakes up, it will help him to see you."

Robyn looked her mother over. Nina appeared utterly exhausted, her usual cheeriness and optimism defeated by the events of the past few days.

"You need something to eat," Robyn told her.

"I haven't been hungry, not since this terrible thing happened to your father..." Nina bent her head as she sat there in the hospital waiting room, as if she simply had no energy left. Even her silvery hair seemed to have lost its luster, falling in limp strands against her cheeks. Always in the past Nina had been the take-charge type, managing the family and the family enterprises with skill and confidence. For Robyn, one of the worst things about this crisis was seeing her mother falter.

"Mom," Robyn said gently. "You really do need to eat something. At least go down to the cafeteria."

Nina stood. "Yes, I suppose I should. But you go to your father, dear."

"Mom...be careful."

"What could happen to me?" Nina asked with a hint of the old spirit. "It's your father we have to be concerned about."

"Just be careful," Robyn said, knowing how inadequate the words sounded. She waited until her mother had stepped onto the elevator. Then she slipped into her father's room, her stomach tightening in apprehension. She'd already undergone the worst, she knew; yesterday she'd had the first shock of seeing how badly hurt her father was. Yet, every time she'd come into the room since, she'd felt disbelief. *That* couldn't be her father, lying so helplessly in the bed, bruised and battered almost beyond recognition. One eye was swollen shut, a deep gash sliced into his cheek, several ribs, as well as his left arm, broken. There had been ominous talk about the possibility of a punctured lung. Although it had turned out to be a false alarm, and although the doctors had patched up Cal Myers as efficiently as possible, a sense of dread still churned inside Robyn. Who had done this to her father? And, dear God, why?

She sank into a chair beside the bed, propping her elbows on her knees. She listened to her father's slow, rasping breath as he slept. Robyn supposed the pain medication had kicked in again. It was a relief to know he could rest.

Robyn gazed at him, hating to see him so vulnerable. Her father had always been such a strong person—confident and decisive. Growing up, she'd known that she could go to him with any problem, and he would have the answer for her. He'd made her feel safe and protected. And, over the years, he'd encouraged *her* to be strong, to have faith in her own abilities. That was one of his most precious gifts to her.

In an echo of her mother's posture a few moments ago, she lowered her head. She felt the prickle of fatigue all through her body, and no wonder—she'd hardly slept at all since arriving in Santa Fe yesterday. She and her mother had taken turns staying with Dad. Aunt Janet and Uncle Greg had taken their own turns, of course, but the entire family was feeling the strain. The night before last, someone had entered Cal Myers's art gallery and brutally attacked him. So far the police had no suspects.

Robyn heard a rustling sound from the bed and glanced up. Her father had awakened and was staring at her. His bruised face had worked into an expression of anguish.

"Dad," she said quickly. "You shouldn't get agitated. That's what the doctors said." She reached to press the buzzer for the nurse, but he took hold of her arm with his free hand. His grip was disconcertingly strong.

"Did you do it?" he asked, laboring to make each word distinct.

"I promise we'll talk about it later. You have to rest—"

"No! Tell me, Robyn. Did you do what I asked?"

She hesitated; but realized he would only grow more upset unless she answered him.

"I don't have one yet, Dad. It takes time, what with filing for a permit and everything. But I went someplace, to see if I actually had it in me. To see if I could actually make myself use a gun...well, I used one, all right. The man at the shooting range told me that my aim was surprisingly good. Those were his exact words, 'surprisingly good.'" She hadn't liked hearing that—it wasn't a talent she wanted to have.

Her father only seemed to grow more distressed, his grip on her arm tightening. "It's not enough! You have to get a gun—now, Robyn. I can't ask your uncle Greg to do it—after his heart attack, he can't take this kind of stress. It has to be you, Robyn. You have to protect your mother. Yourself."

"Tell me *why*, Dad," she said, starting to feel frantic. "Who attacked you? What makes you think they'll come after us, too? Give me something to go by—"

"Just do it. Before it's too late." His hand finally loosened from her arm, falling back on the bed.

"Dad, the police will be questioning you again. Tell them what you know...tell them exactly what happened. If you're really worried about Mom or me being in danger, you have to tell the police—"

"No." The despair in his voice was raw. "I can't. I was warned not to involve the police. If I do, something even worse will happen. And you mustn't tell your mother! Not a word about the gun. Just get it, and watch over her. Do you understand, Robyn?"

A chill seeped through her. "I don't understand anything," she whispered. "Oh, Dad, why can't you trust me enough to tell me the truth?"

She might as well not have spoken. Already he had slipped back into that drugged sleep, leaving her with all questions unanswered. How quickly the life of her family had shattered out of its normal, ordinary routine. The vicious, unexplained attack on her father...the distraught phone call from her mother...Robyn's last-minute flight out of Denver...and then her father's frightening demand. *Get a gun, Robyn. You have to do this. Get a gun, and protect your mother. Protect yourself. Promise me that you'll do exactly as I say.*

At last she'd promised. How could she have refused him anything as he lay there hurting? How could she ignore the fact that danger suddenly threatened her family? But a gun…

She hated guns—she hated violence. As a high-school teacher, she'd seen too many kids get caught up in violence. She'd told her students over and over that it was never an answer to any problem. Yet, this very afternoon, she'd gone into that shooting range, driven by her promise to her father. She'd been driven, too, by anger and frustration and by the unreasoning conviction that perhaps it really *was* up to her to keep anything terrible from happening again. She'd held a gun in her hand and fired it, and tried desperately to believe she could keep herself and her family safe.

But then Mark Stewart had sat her down in that chair and told her she was scared, almost sounding as if he was accusing her. He'd been all too perceptive, that much was certain, and Robyn had immediately gone on the defensive with him.

Now she went restlessly to the window and looked out. A brilliant New Mexico sky arched above, tinged gold from the late-afternoon sun. She told herself there was no sky like it anywhere else, stretching limitlessly over mountain and mesa.

She tried to concentrate only on the beauty of it, tried to give herself some measure of peace. The effort was useless.

A nurse came into the room to check on her father, and Robyn went back to the waiting area. She sat down and leafed futilely through a magazine. A few moments later her mother stepped off the elevator, carrying two plastic cups of coffee.

"Is he all right?" Nina asked breathlessly. "Maybe I shouldn't have left—"

"He's fine." Robyn paused. Her father had been so adamant—*Don't tell your mother. Just watch over her.* But didn't Nina have a right to know as much as possible? "Mom…he did wake up for a few moments. And he said he was worried about us."

Nina attempted a smile. She sank into a chair beside Robyn and handed her a cup. "That sounds just like your father. He's always done his best to take care of us. I'm sure he can't bear the thought of us taking care of *him.*"

Robyn sipped her coffee without really tasting it. She marveled that even in a time of crisis familiar patterns asserted themselves. Cal Myers was a man of vision and imagination. He knew how to see the hidden talent in the work of fledgling artists, knew how to encourage that talent and make it flower. He'd helped many, many artists go on to prestigious careers, and in the process developed his own reputation. He was not, however, a man who liked to concern himself with the day-to-day requirements of running a business or a family. Nina was the one who'd taken care of the Myers clan over the years. She'd always kept things going—ensuring that investments were well maintained, bills paid, obligations met. Even so, she perpetuated the illusion that her husband was looking after things.

"Mom, Dad thinks we might be in danger. You…and me."

Some of Nina's usual matter-of-factness seemed to reassert itself. "That's nonsense," she said. "An awful thing happened to your father, but it's over. It was something horribly random. Someone breaking in, trying to rob the gallery. We need better security, that's all."

"Nothing was stolen," Robyn said, still speaking as gently as possible. "All those valuable paintings, and not a single one is missing."

Nina's expression grew stubborn. "Your father is a brave man. He stopped whoever it was before anything *could* be stolen."

"Robbery wasn't necessarily the motive," Robyn persisted. "The police said there were no signs of a break-in. Maybe Dad let the attacker—or attackers—into the gallery."

Nina gave a frown. "What are you implying, Robyn? That your father would be foolish enough to open the door to suspicious strangers, when it was practically the middle of the night?"

"Maybe we're not talking about strangers. Maybe he opened the door to someone he knew."

"Your father would never associate with...with *criminals*," Nina said. "And only a criminal could have attacked him in that savage way." Nina's loyalty to her husband was impressive; her entire life seemed to revolve around Cal Myers. How awful it must be for her, knowing that someone had assaulted him in his very own gallery. But the questions could not be evaded.

"Mom, why was Dad at the gallery so late? That doesn't make any sense, either."

"He often works late," Nina replied. "That's part of being self-employed. A stranger broke in and attacked him. We're just lucky that your father's going to be all right." Despite the firmness of her voice, worry lines had etched into her face, along with the telltale lines of age. Nina had recently turned sixty. While still a pretty woman, today she showed every single one of her years. Robyn reached over and clasped her hand.

"Mom, you have to listen to me. I don't want anything to happen to you. If Dad thinks you're in danger, then he has a reason. Even if he won't tell us what it is—"

Nina withdrew her hand. "Your father would not deceive us. He's already told the police that he doesn't know who attacked him. He has undergone an ordeal. All he needs from us right now is our support."

Robyn saw her mother's shuttered expression. This was Nina all over again, refusing to admit that her successful, talented, charismatic husband could be anything less than perfect, anything less than aboveboard. Robyn, however, had to be a little more realistic. Much as she admired and loved her father, she believed that he was hiding something. Why else his demand that she obtain a gun?

Robyn was on the verge of telling her mother about Cal's urgent request. *You have to do it, Robyn. You have to protect your mother, and yourself…*

But there was the other part of the request to consider. He had been so insistent that she *not* tell her mother. Why? Always that question, over and over, resonating in Robyn's mind.

"Robyn," said her mother, "everything has been so chaotic we haven't even had a chance to talk. I want you to tell me about Denver, about the high school and all the rest of it." Obviously Nina would rather make small talk than confront any uncomfortable discussions about her husband's plight.

"Mom," she said, "about teaching…the fact is, I'm considering taking a leave of absence. I'm not sure it's what I want to do anymore."

"Nonsense, dear. You've always loved your job so much. And you do so much good—"

"It doesn't seem that way," Robyn said heavily. "I don't feel like I'm making a difference at all. There are lots of reasons—"

"Oh, honey." Nina patted her shoulder. "Of course you make a difference. You know what's wrong? You're just getting over a divorce, and of course that's traumatic. I'm sure it tends to color the rest of your life, and you mustn't let it."

"My second divorce," Robyn couldn't help reminding her. But it wasn't a comfortable thing to admit. Not once, but twice in her life, Robyn had fallen for the wrong man. She now had two ex-husbands as proof of her dubious judgment. "Anyway," she went on, "my personal life doesn't have anything to do with teaching—"

"Give it time," Nina said consolingly. "Another man will come along. This time he'll be the right one."

Robyn would have laughed if she'd had any energy for it. Her mother, the perennial optimist. The fact that her only child couldn't stay married didn't seem to daunt her in the least. And Nina persisted in believing that true happiness could only be found in partnership with a man. Didn't her own life with Cal Myers prove as much? Forty years of marriage...forty years of devotion, forty years of believing that nothing really bad or unpleasant could ever occur. But now something bad *had* occurred, to Nina's very own husband.

Nina rose from her chair, her attention already retreating from Robyn. "I need to be with your father. Everything will be all right...as long as I'm there with him. I just have to be there."

Robyn watched her mother go down the corridor. Then she stood and walked the length of the waiting room, the turmoil inside her threatening to overflow. It struck her that every aspect of her life was in disarray. The inescapable doubts about her career, the debacle of divorce number two...and now this, her father lying defenseless in a hospital bed, unseen danger threatening her family. Robyn clasped her arms tightly against her body, but that didn't stop the sensation engulfing her—the sensation that, any moment, she would shatter completely.

CHAPTER TWO

MARK READ the notice in the newspaper for possibly the third time, telling himself it had to be some other Kerry Stewart. Yeah, right, he mocked himself. There had to be a lot of twenty-one-year-old girls with his daughter's name, announcing their engagements in the *Santa Fe Gazette*.

Mark held up the engagement notice, studying the picture that accompanied it. It was his daughter, all right—and she looked so mature, so sure of herself. She also looked very happy, clinging to the arm of a spindly young man Mark had never seen before. Frederick Graham, the paper said, a recent graduate from the University of New Mexico with a degree in finance. Who the hell got a degree in *finance?* The kid didn't even sound as if he had a job yet. And why the hell was his daughter marrying some guy named Frederick? What was she going to end up calling him? Fred—or, even worse, Freddie?

Mark knew what was really bugging him: the fact that his youngest daughter was getting married and she hadn't even bothered to let him know. The sensation he felt now went way beyond regret. Had he failed his children so completely that this was how it had to be? Reading about them in the newspaper instead of being a part of their lives?

Someone stepped into the office. Still immersed in painful thoughts of his daughters, he glanced up reluctantly. A woman stood before him...the woman who'd come by yesterday, wanting to learn how to shoot a gun. Hazel eyes, reddish hair that curled just a bit against her cheeks, name of Robyn Myers. She was still beautiful. And something told him she was still scared.

He nodded at the chair in front of the desk. "Have a seat," he said.

"Don't you think you're pushing things a little with your friend Benjamin?" She glanced around the small office.

"Benjamin's glad for some vacation time. But I didn't think I'd see you again, Ms. Myers."

"Why not?"

"Maybe I'm wrong, but you didn't seem to like coming here."

Even now, he had the feeling she was about to turn and walk out of the place. After a moment, though, she sat down. Her hair was a little rumpled, as if she'd driven over here with the windows rolled down, allowing the breeze full rein with her. She held her hands loosely in her lap, obviously trying to disguise her tension. Her eyes were shadowed by any number of emotions.

She sat there and gazed at him as if she still couldn't figure out what she was doing here.

He glanced down at the newspaper. "My daughter's getting married," he said.

"Congratulations," Robyn said.

"Don't be too happy for me. If I hadn't been catching up on the local news, I wouldn't even have known. It's not like she sent me an announcement herself or anything."

Robyn Myers didn't answer, nor did she look sympathetic.

"My daughters have a stepfather they call Dad. Nobody to blame but myself, though. I guess you could say I haven't been the most involved father."

Robyn Myers continued to appear less than sympathetic. As far as he was concerned, that made her a good audience.

"My ex-wife says I was a lousy father even before the divorce. She says my job was always more important to me than my family. So she remarried, and provided a stepfather my kids seem to worship." That was the hardest thing for Mark to admit—that his efforts to be a better father over the years had been met by his kids' undoubted preference for their stepdad. "Now I just keep asking myself—is it too late to make things right? And who the hell do I think I am, imagining that I *can* make things right?''

Robyn didn't seem to have any answer for these questions, but she'd settled back in her chair.

"I wonder why I'm telling you any of this," he said dryly.

"I don't know," she remarked. "Maybe you think I'll be encouraged by your…candor. Maybe you think I'll open up in return, and tell you what's wrong."

He nodded thoughtfully. "Any chance of that?"

She stared down at her hands, and now they tightened in her lap. She took a ragged breath. "I only came here so I could have another lesson," she said.

"Are you sure that's the only reason?"

Her head came up. "*Yes*, Mr. Stewart. Much as I'm fascinated by your personal travails, that's all I want—to learn how to shoot."

He folded the newspaper and set it to one side. Then he led her back to the shooting range. He set the target again, got her positioned with the automatic. She was definitely a natural; she remembered everything he'd taught her yesterday, holding the gun straight out in front of her with absolute steadiness. This time she didn't try to squint. She looked down the sight as if imagining exactly where the bullet would hit.

Just like yesterday, however, she didn't shoot

right away. She stood there with her feet angled slightly apart, her shoulders set in a tense, rigid line. And then, almost convulsively, her finger pulled back on the trigger.

She didn't stop there. She held on to the gun and aimed one bullet after another at the bull's-eye. The expression on her face was one of absolute fury and pain. He had seen that look before, with people who felt trapped and panicked. Shot after shot she fired. He knew better than to touch her or try to calm her. He just let her empty the clip. She had started to shake, but her finger seemed to move with a will of its own on the trigger.

Even when she'd run out of bullets, her finger kept pressing the trigger. Only after a moment did she loosen her grip and drop the gun. She yanked off the sound dampeners and tossed those aside also. When she turned, the look she gave Mark was one of horror and dismay. Then, tears brimming in her eyes, she fled from the shooting range.

ROBYN LEANED FORWARD and put her head against the steering wheel. Her cheeks were wet, but she barely took note of the fact. She didn't care that she'd made a fool of herself in front of Mark Stewart. That seemed inconsequential. The way she'd felt when she'd held the gun—that was tormenting her.

What was wrong with her—where had the terrible rage inside her come from?

She closed her eyes, but the tears kept coming. She felt herself trembling.

There was a tap at her window. Reluctantly she opened her eyes and saw that Mark Stewart had followed her. She rolled down the window a fraction.

"Please leave me alone," she said through clenched teeth.

He didn't argue with her. He just opened her door, took hold of her elbow and deftly maneuvered her from the car. She tried to resist him, but he wouldn't let go. Before she knew it, he'd guided her across the parking lot to a sturdy old Land Cruiser. The tears continued to spill onto her cheeks no matter how often she wiped them away. Mark opened the passenger door and put her inside, even reaching across to fasten her seat belt. Then he walked around the vehicle and climbed in the driver's side.

"I wish...I wish you'd just leave me alone," she said.

"It's not hard to see something's troubling you," he said imperturbably. "You came back today because you needed to talk to someone. I'm a good listener. So that's what we're going to do. You're going to talk, and I'm going to listen." He started the engine and pulled out of the parking lot.

"I don't want to go anywhere with you," she began.

"I'm not kidnapping you, Ms. Myers. I'm just taking you down to my favorite coffee shop. We're going to sit in a booth...perhaps have a doughnut or two...and perhaps you'll tell me what has you running scared."

Five minutes later they were, indeed, sitting in the booth of a small coffee shop. Mark had placed their order, and it arrived promptly: steaming mugs of coffee and two large cinnamon rolls. Robyn couldn't have imagined that she'd ever feel hungry again, but the cinnamon roll enticed her.

"Take a bite," Mark said. "A good bite."

"Do you always commandeer people this way?" she asked irritably. The tears had finally stopped and she'd blotted her face with a tissue, but her eyes ached and still threatened to leak at the corners.

"I do what's necessary," Mark said. "Right now it's necessary to feed you."

She tore off a small piece of cinnamon roll, nibbled a bite or two. She worked on another piece, then a little more. Before she knew it, she'd eaten half the roll. Then she sat with her hands wrapped around her mug of coffee. She gave Mark a grudging look, wondering why she'd allowed him to take over like this. He seemed the type of man who was used to taking over. She searched for flaws in him.

By no means could he be called a conventionally handsome man. He had too many rough edges for that—a face that looked as if it had seen too much, dark untidy hair, gray eyes, which she suspected could all too easily turn cold and hard. Mark Stewart gave the impression that he would be able to handle himself in any situation. It struck Robyn then: no matter how strong her father had always seemed to her, if Mark had been the one in that art gallery, and an attacker had entered, the outcome would have been much different. She gave an involuntary shiver.

"Mind telling me about it?" Mark said.

She took a spoon and stirred her coffee. "I hate what happened back there," she said in a low voice. "At the shooting range…the way I felt…"

"Like you could kill someone?"

Robyn pushed the coffee away. "No! Yes…I wasn't thinking coherently. Everything seemed to descend on me all at once. The anxiety of these last few days…and everything else, too. The frustrations I've been having with my teaching career…oh, Lord, even my ex-husband." She pressed her hands against the table. "I picked up that gun, and everything engulfed me. I wasn't in control, don't you see? I started firing the damned thing, filled with that anger. I didn't know I could be like that. So…so…"

"Out of control?" Mark suggested.

She closed her eyes briefly, the shame of those

few moments haunting her. "Worse than uncontrolled. It was...unreasoning. Just all that hateful anger. I couldn't stop. I didn't know how to stop." Miserably, she opened her eyes. Mark Stewart was regarding her calmly.

"Look at it this way," he said. "You didn't take the gun and try to hurt somebody else. You shot at a target. You didn't turn your anger anyplace it could do harm. Deep down, you *were* in control, you were thinking."

She wanted desperately to believe the logic of his words, but she couldn't forget the way she'd felt. "I didn't know a human being could ever feel that vengeful," she muttered.

"Is it your ex-husband?" Mark asked almost conversationally. "Is he the reason you wanted to learn how to shoot?"

"My ex-husband..." She gave a bleak laugh. "Brad and I may not get along anymore, but he's not capable of driving me to violence." She looked at Mark, saw the expression in his eyes that seemed to say nothing in this world could surprise him. Suddenly she found herself telling him everything.

"Three nights ago someone came into my father's art gallery and attacked him. It was vicious and seemingly senseless. Except that now my father's in the hospital, and he's made me promise to get a gun. He thinks whoever did it will come after my mother, or me. He won't say why. And he won't tell the police what really happened. Today, when I held that gun…I really wanted to hurt the person who hurt my father.''

She had run out of words. The problem was still hers; it hadn't gone away. But she'd shared it with someone who didn't seem about to go into shock or fly off the handle. No…Mark Stewart definitely wasn't the type who'd fly off the handle.

His expression had grown intent. ''Was anything stolen from your father's art gallery?''

''Nothing. That's just it—there were no signs of a break-in, not a single painting stolen. They're quite valuable paintings, yet they didn't even tempt who-ever attacked my father. There has to be another reason for what happened, but Dad won't say what it is. He just seems so…so *distraught*. I don't know how to explain it, except that he's suffering in spirit as much as he is physically. That's not like him at all.''

''Robyn,'' Mark said, ''has your father ever had any enemies? Not just recently—I want you to think back. Anything from the past, anything at all that might indicate someone with a grievance against him.''

She considered his question for several moments, but finally shook her head. ''My father is one of the most generous people you'll ever meet. Although he's a talented artist himself, he prefers to focus on other people's careers. He's helped any number of artists to make names for themselves, and they're all very grateful to him. He has friends, not enemies. I can't think of anyone who'd wish him harm—for any reason. That's what's so puzzling.''

"He runs an art gallery...any chance he could be involved in something illegal? Forgery, for example."

"Of course not!" she said defensively. "I know my father. He couldn't possibly do something illegal. He doesn't have it in him."

"Maybe you don't know your father as well as you think. Obviously there's something he's not telling you. Obviously he has at least one enemy—a pretty serious one, at that."

Robyn stared at Mark. "Do you always look so quickly for the underside of things?"

"Occupational hazard, I guess." He drank some of his coffee. "I'm a detective."

She struggled to understand. "Like a private detective, you mean?"

"Police. Homicide, to be exact."

She stared at him. "I don't get it. You teach at a shooting range."

"Temporarily. I'm on leave from the department—recovering from a tussle with a bullet. Nothing too serious...but my boss thought I needed a little extra downtime." Mark gave a slight grimace. Robyn, however, wasn't interested right now in any problems he had with his boss. She stood up, only to find that she was shaking again.

"Thanks for the coffee, Mr. Stewart," she said, surprised at how normal her voice sounded. "And the cinnamon roll, too, of course. But maybe you'll understand why I can't stay and chat. My father has made it very clear that involving the police any further could be dangerous for my entire family. Goodbye." Robyn walked out of the coffee shop, the door swinging shut behind her.

She was halfway down the street before he caught up to her.

"Robyn," he said. "Never listen to anyone who tells you not to go to the police."

"What's this, Mr. Stewart—a little P.R. work for the department? You're not exactly unbiased, are you?"

"The police are the only people who *can* help you."

"Fine," she said. "I'll take that under advisement. But you said you were on leave from the department, didn't you? So, officially, I don't have to tell you a damn thing." She quickened her pace. In response he lengthened his stride easily.

"Okay, you're ticked because I didn't happen to mention I was a cop the first time we met."

"It does seem you've been operating under false pretenses," she said acidly.

"I have a habit of following my instincts," he told her. "They warned me that you wouldn't talk to me at all if you thought I was a policeman."

She had a wild desire to run. Instead, she forced herself to talk to him. "Your instincts are highly accurate. What are they telling you now?"

"That you need somebody to help you. That you want to trust me, but you're still scared. That you know you should trust me."

Suddenly she stopped walking. She leaned against the side of a building.

"Mark," she said. "I don't know anything for certain. Maybe my father's right. Maybe talking to the police is the surest way to bring more harm on my family. Or maybe *not* talking to the police could be our biggest mistake. I don't know. All I know is that I haven't slept at all the last few days, I haven't eaten much except half a cinnamon roll and...I'd just like to be on my own for a little while."

"Robyn...you need help."

"Let me guess," she said. "You have a little spare time on your hands, nothing much going on down at the shooting range."

"Maybe my motives aren't so bad," he answered. "Maybe this is the kind of thing I do on the job.

Maybe it's the kind of thing I've been missing. And maybe I just want to help.''

He made it sound as if she'd be doing him a favor by leaning on his shoulder. Granted, it appeared to be a broad, competent shoulder, and she was sorely tempted to lean. But she couldn't forget her father's warning. *Don't tell anyone, Robyn. Don't involve the police.* She'd already gone way too far by opening up to Mark Stewart.

Purposely avoiding any glance in Mark's direction, she began walking again. ''Look, I'm sorry you're…laid off from your job—''

''On temporary leave,'' he reminded her as he kept pace.

''Anyway,'' Robyn said, walking a little faster, ''two very nice police officers talked to my father in the hospital. If necessary, I'll contact them.''

With just a touch on her arm, he compelled her to stop. ''Look,'' he said. ''What I told you before is true. I miss doing my job. I've been going damn stir-crazy during my so-called recuperation. There'd be nothing wrong with me providing a little unofficial help on your case.''

The anger flared in her again. ''Is that how you look at people—as *cases?* Someone's life is falling apart, but meanwhile it's just an interesting *case* for you to solve—''

''It's what I'm good at, Robyn,'' he said quietly.

"Personal relationships...yeah, I'm lousy at those. But work is something else."

She felt saddened by his words. Mark Stewart seemed to have closed himself off in some essential way, focusing only on the job that was so important to him. But her instincts warned her that she had to handle this on her own. For her parents' sake, she had to be strong. Until she knew more, she had to listen to her father's warning. It might be the only way to keep her family safe.

"No, Mark," she said. "Just...no. I can't accept your help."

CHAPTER THREE

MARK HAD CHOSEN the best restaurant in town. At least, he thought it was the best restaurant in town. He wasn't all that sure what his daughter would think. The place was small, low-key, on a narrow winding lane some distance from the plaza. The adobe walls had been plastered thickly over the past century or so, the layers swirled like frosting on a cake. Overhead the time-weathered beams known as *vigas* had been left exposed, and the deep-set window frames had been trimmed in a satisfying blue-green color. It was the food, of course, that gave the place its reputation, an offering of dishes unabashedly southwestern: green-chile stew, blue-corn soup, pinto-bean pie.

Mark sat at a table in one of the window alcoves, nursing a tequila sour. He could no longer deny that his daughter was late. Not exactly eager to see the old man, it seemed. When he'd called and asked her to join him for lunch, her voice had been decidedly cool over the phone. She'd agreed only with reluctance.

He shifted in his seat, trying to get comfortable. Some days his leg ached more than others. Lord, at forty-three maybe he really *was* starting to feel his years.

He shifted again, easing his leg out in front of him. Maybe it had been the wrong approach, inviting Kerry to a restaurant for dinner. Maybe he should have tried for something a little more casual and relaxed. But wasn't that the problem right there? He hadn't been casual or relaxed with either of his daughters in a very long while. Both of them treated him as if he was some sort of inconvenient relative—like a distant uncle they had to be polite to.

Did he have anyone to blame but himself? Sure, his ex-wife had played her part—after the divorce, she'd found plenty of subtle little ways to keep his daughters occupied and away from him. Perhaps it had been her payback for all the years when he'd been a distant husband. But there was no point in allocating blame. Only one question remained: Where the hell did he go from here?

He signaled the waiter. "Any calls for me?"

"No, Mr. Stewart. Still no calls."

Thinking about his daughters made him feel a failure. He far preferred the way his job made him feel—convinced that he was making a contribution, doing something useful. Getting back on the job, that was what he needed. Being assigned a case, following leads, working out the puzzle set before him. Lord, he missed that right now. And, because he missed it, he'd done some unofficial poking into the Cal Myers case. Forget the fact that this morning Robyn Myers had categorically refused his help. Mark had gone right ahead and put in a few calls to the station house, gotten the update on Robyn's father. It was pretty much as she'd said. Cal Myers claimed to have been attacked by someone he didn't know—someone he'd never even seen before. No, he couldn't provide any description. The attacker had been wearing a mask, and it had all happened very quickly. No, he didn't have anything else to tell the police.

But meanwhile, according to Robyn, Cal Myers had asked her to get a gun. And he seemed afraid that whoever had attacked him would next turn on his daughter, or his wife. His fears were something that couldn't be dismissed.

This morning Mark had given Robyn a few pointers on looking out for herself, advice that would probably do her a whole lot more good than a gun. Little things, like making sure she didn't go anyplace alone, and always being aware of what was happening around her. There was a certain watchfulness that became second nature if you practiced it long enough, a watchfulness that would keep you out of the most basic kinds of trouble.

"Hello, Father. You're a million miles away, as usual."

Mark rose to his feet and gazed at his daughter.

She looked so polished, so poised, nothing like the little girl who had once loved to play softball and skin her knees in the dirt. This Kerry wore an expensive silk dress. Her hair was swept up in some kind of twist, saved from bland sophistication by a brightly beaded clasp stuck in as if at the last minute. Mark smiled a little. Kerry had a habit of dressing conservatively, but then she'd add some colorful, individual detail that would betray a rebellious spirit. He wished she would let the rebellion out more often. It was what made her unique and special, her ability to see when the rules ought to be broken.

Now Mark wondered how to greet her. He supposed that most fathers would give their daughters a kiss on the cheek, but tonight Kerry had a don't-touch air about her. A handshake? You didn't shake hands with your kids, not if you were on speaking terms.

"You look great," he said inadequately. "I guess being engaged agrees with you."

"Frederick and I are both very happy." The response was automatic, no doubt the standard reply she tossed off for strangers and acquaintances. Mark pulled out a chair for her and a few seconds later they were sitting across from each other at the table. Kerry ordered a brandy cocktail, and then gave Mark a reassuring glance.

"I am twenty-one, you know. I'm allowed to drink."

"Of course." He'd worked hard six months ago to find just the right gift for her coming-of-age birthday—a silver and turquoise necklace that had set him back a month's salary. She'd accepted it the way she'd accepted all his birthday presents over the years—with a friendly but careless thank-you. It was as if she couldn't even bother to be angry with him; he'd become that insignificant in her life.

"Kerry," he said, "it's…great that you're getting married. Really great."

"If you say 'great' one more time, you'll make it sound like it's not so great, after all." Now there was just the slightest edge to her voice.

"I guess I'm still having trouble getting used to the idea," he said. "It seems like only yesterday…"

"I know. It seems like only yesterday I was a little girl in pigtails."

"You never wore pigtails," he said. "You hated them."

"Really? Imagine you remembering something like that." She opened her menu and began to peruse it. "I've never eaten here before, but I hear the food's good."

Mark rubbed the back of his neck. They could go on like this all night, exchanging meaningless comments. Or they could be real with each other for once.

"Kerry," he said, "when I saw that announcement in the paper...it really hit me. How far apart we've grown."

She didn't even glance up from her menu. "We see each other all the time," she said.

"Every few months or so. That's not all the time."

Usually when he called his daughters, they had some excuse why they couldn't see him. Get-togethers with their *real* family, previous commitments with friends. They were always civil about it, always gracious, promising that next time things would work out. Mark would tell himself how glad he was that his kids were busy and happy. But then he would let more and more weeks go by before he contacted either of them again. Was he worried that one of these times they'd reject him for good? Or was he just proving his ex-wife right, after all—he didn't know how to put family first? Either way, he knew that he hadn't tried hard enough to break down the barriers between himself and his children.

"I'd like things to change," he said. "I'd like us to see each other more often. I know I've been at fault—"

"It's not anybody's fault," Kerry said hurriedly. "I spend most of my time in Albuquerque these days, what with school."

"Albuquerque's not very far away at all," Mark said. "We should be able to work something out."

"We're having dinner together now, aren't we? Hmm...I haven't had *posole* in a while."

Obviously she wasn't going to let him apologize for his failure to keep in closer contact. Maybe that was the ultimate brush-off, letting your father know that you would not dignify his regrets by giving them any attention whatsoever.

He tried a different tack. "How is school, anyway?"

"Fine. I'm taking a wonderful writing class. I think it's really helping me to branch out."

He wasn't too sure what she meant by "branch out," but it didn't seem appropriate to ask. "Still writing poetry?" he ventured instead.

"Of course."

How did he talk about his daughter's poetry, especially when she'd evaded all his requests to see some of it?

For all he knew, she was a brilliant writer. Too bad she wouldn't let him find out.

Just then a young man approached their table with a confident stride. Kerry lifted her face to the man, and he kissed her. It took Mark a couple of seconds to recognize this guy as the one in the engagement photo—none other than Frederick Graham, college graduate in finance.

"I asked Frederick to meet us here," Kerry said. "I hope you don't mind—I just thought you'd welcome the opportunity to meet him."

Mark shook hands with his daughter's fiancé. This wasn't what he'd had in mind at all. He'd wanted some time alone with Kerry so the two of them could finally start talking to each other. She'd expertly thwarted *that* attempt.

"Mr. Stewart," said Frederick Graham, "it's an honor to meet you."

Honor? Since when was it an honor to meet your girlfriend's father? The guy was laying it on a little thick.

Not only that, but Mark didn't like the looks of him. He seemed too damn young, for one thing, with the gangly limbs of someone who hadn't fully settled into himself. How could he be a college graduate when he looked as if another growth spurt was just around the corner?

All three of them ordered dinner, and then Frederick Graham gave Mark an overly assured smile. "Sir, I understand you're with the police. Must be a fascinating career. I'd like to hear all about it."

Sir? Now it was *sir?* "Why don't we talk about your plans instead," Mark suggested. Even from across the table, he saw the way his daughter stiffened. But he was only trying to find out if this...this youngster would end up having a decent job.

Kerry was the one who jumped in. "A lot of firms want to hire Frederick. He's in a very good position."

Frederick grinned, and put his arm around her. "Let's not exaggerate, Kerry. I have a few decent prospects, Mr. Stewart. Rest assured, I'll be able to support your daughter."

"Kerry, fortunately, believes in supporting herself," Mark said. He thought for sure he'd score points with that one—the enlightened father, expecting his daughter to make her own way as a woman. Turned out he was wrong.

"Frederick doesn't have any problem with the fact that I won't be making a lot of money," Kerry said. "Or maybe not any money at first. As soon as I get my degree, I'll be writing poetry full-time."

"Poetry...full-time? What happened to your internship with the publishing house?" Mark asked.

"Oh, I quit that ages ago. Poetry is what I've always wanted to do. Frederick is behind me a hundred percent."

"You'd better believe it, Mr. Stewart. It's my prediction that someday Kerry is going to be a very well-known and respected writer."

His daughter, the poetess. Most likely the penniless poetess. Mark wondered if Kerry had thought this through. Did she expect to keep up her expensive taste in clothes, her love of travel? Not to mention little things like *eating*. Now Mark wondered what his ex-wife had to say about all this. Andrea couldn't be overjoyed that her future son-in-law didn't even have a job yet—and that her youngest daughter was going to devote herself solely to poetry.

The conversation was dying, and Mark made an effort to prod it back to life. "So," he said, "how did you two meet?" He couldn't think of a safer question, but Kerry frowned.

"It's too involved a story, and I'm sure you're not really interested—"

"I'll tell it," intervened Frederick. "It happened at school, Mr. Stewart. Kerry was studying really hard for an exam in psychology, and she fell asleep at the library. That's the first time I saw her—fast asleep with her head on the desk, and she was actually snoring. A very delicate snore. Pretty endearing, actually—"

"Frederick. You don't have to go into this much *detail*." Kerry seemed to be growing tense. Her fiancé, however, cheerfully ignored her, and went on at length about the fated meeting at the library and a subsequent rendezvous at the student union. All Mark had to do was sit back and listen.

Frederick Graham seemed perfectly content to ramble on, heedless of Kerry's discomfort. Mark saw the way she creased her napkin over and over, the way she glanced toward the door as if longing to escape. And he knew there was something more going on here...something more than mere embarrassment over having the details of their courtship revealed. Maybe this engagement wasn't going as well as Kerry insisted. Maybe she wasn't really that happy with Frederick Graham. Mark didn't like the thought of his daughter not being happy, for any reason. He found himself scowling at the boy, enough so that Frederick began to wind down.

"Well, sir...anyway, that's how I met Kerry, and we've been together ever since. I promise you I'll do everything in my power to make her glad she agreed to be my wife." The kid was definitely laying it on thick. Kerry seemed to agree; she scooted her chair just a little bit away from Frederick. That didn't faze him. He managed to lean toward her, keeping his arm draped around her shoulders. Again she scooted her chair away.

"Sweetie, you okay?" Frederick asked.

"I'm fine," Kerry muttered. "I wish—I just wish the food would come."

"You don't seem okay," Frederick insisted. "You seem a little uptight. You can tell us what's wrong. I mean, you're here among friends—"

"Stop." Kerry pushed back her chair and stood. Two bright spots of color burned in her cheeks, and she seemed about to cry. She looked from Mark to Frederick then back again. "This was a mistake," she said. "A very big mistake. Seeing the two of you together, side by side...the man I'm supposed to marry, and my *father*...it makes me wonder if I even want to go through with the wedding!"

For once Frederick seemed to lose his assurance. He stared at Kerry. "What are you talking about?" he asked. "I know you've been nervous about getting married, but that's natural. I'm nervous, too. Why can't we just be nervous together?"

She clenched the back of her chair. "It's more than that. Something's been bothering me, and I didn't even know what it was." Kerry gave Mark an accusing glance, after which she gave her fiancé an accusing glance. "Then you came in, and it all clicked. I saw exactly what could happen...how easily it could happen. The two of us getting married, Frederick, but ending up exactly like my mother and *him*. Unhappy and miserable and *divorced*. I can't let it happen! Don't you see? I just can't let it happen." The tears spilled over. Kerry suddenly seemed aware of the people at other tables who were trying not to watch her. With a small cry, she turned and made her escape.

Mark rose to go after her. He didn't know how

to offer her comfort, but he had to try. Frederick, however, shook his head. "It's better if I take care of it, sir. She'll talk to me when we're alone, and she'll tell me what's really going on. I'm sorry about what she said just now. She didn't mean it, you know. I'm sure we'll get it cleared up in no time. Anyway, very nice meeting you, sir." Frederick pumped Mark's hand, his smile forced this time, and then he loped after Kerry.

Mark sank back into his chair. For a minute there he'd almost felt sorry for Frederick Graham. The kid was trying so damn hard to make everything right: portray himself as the mature adult with everything under control, get along with his fiancée's father, smooth over his fiancée's outburst. That was a lot of work for one person.

The waiter arrived bearing a tray with three plates of food, and gave Mark an inquiring look.

"Change in plans," Mark said. "But go ahead, set it down—I'm paying for everything."

He'd been paying for his mistakes a long time, it seemed. Years ago, when his daughters had been younger, he'd believed firmly and idealistically in the value of his work—chasing down the bad guy, trying to make the world a little bit safer. That had meant days and nights away from home, absorbed in one case after another. It had also meant efforts to keep his family remote from the inevitable seediness and harshness of his job. And, in the process, he'd ended up keeping the people he loved remote from himself...

He gazed at the three plates of untouched food now set before him. One fact alone seemed paramount: His youngest daughter was unhappy, and he was the cause.

ROBYN PACED through the art gallery one more time. A few paintings were propped against the wall. She tipped one toward her and peered at its backside. Nothing unusual—just ordinary framing, with the canvas stretched over it. Certainly there was no clue that would explain the vicious attack on her father. She felt a bit foolish. What had she hoped for—a note left behind by the perpetrator, conveniently explaining everything? But she'd combed the gallery over and over, searching for something, anything, that would help her understand. She hated the helplessness of *not* knowing.

A knock came at the door, startling her. She'd made sure everything was locked and bolted after letting herself in, reassuring herself that she would be quite safe that way. Now she went to the door and peered warily through the glass. She saw Mark Stewart standing outside.

She hesitated a few seconds, then unlocked the door and swung it open.

"Hello," Mark said.

"I don't suppose it's any surprise," she said, "you managing to find me. Doing your detective work, are you?"

He stepped inside the gallery and glanced around. "You told me you wouldn't go anywhere alone. Now here you are, back at the scene of the crime."

She folded her arms against her body. "Why did you come here, Mark? I told you that I would be very careful, and I have been. I'm practically developing eyes in the back of my head, making sure no one sneaks up on me unawares."

"I guess I expected you to come for another lesson today. You turned down my help, but I figured you might want a few more pointers on handling a gun. When you didn't make it to the shooting range, I got a little concerned."

"I've decided to pass on buying a gun," she said. "After my experience yesterday…it just seems like it's not for me."

"You didn't do anything wrong," he told her. "Okay, you got mad, but you took it out on the bull's-eye. You didn't lose control."

"I *felt* out of control, that was bad enough." She didn't feel particularly on top of the situation right now, and that bothered her. For some reason Mark's presence in her father's art gallery was too uncomfortably dominating, too unsettlingly potent. Perhaps it was his sureness, his way of assuming command. Perhaps it was also his dark hair, his definite features, his unequivocal masculinity. But did he really think he could come in here and take over, the way he'd done yesterday when she'd lost it at the shooting range? Couldn't he stop being a police detective, not even for a minute?

She looked around the gallery, trying to regain some equilibrium. This was a large, airy place, striking in its simplicity. All superfluous details had been pared away so that only the work of the artists would stand out. The floors were a glossy oak, the walls a clean white. Several of the paintings displayed were evocative southwestern landscapes: a field of chile peppers glowing red in the afternoon sun, aspens turning to gold in the Sandia Mountains, a view of multitiered Taos Pueblo. There were a few stark portraits and other paintings in a bold abstract style. Altogether it was a startling but effective mix.

"Dad's always been one to take chances," she murmured, almost to herself.

"Maybe he took a chance he shouldn't have," Mark suggested, "and that's why someone beat him up."

Robyn felt a murky swirl of anger and irritation that Mark Stewart seemed to inspire in her. "I meant that he takes chances on artists. He'll see the potential in someone's work, when no one else can see it. He'll gamble on that person's talent, and usually he wins.''

Mark didn't answer, but his expression was skeptical. He looked around the gallery one more time, as if he would find some secret she hadn't revealed to him.

''Thinking the worst about people,'' she said. ''That's what you do, isn't it?''

His gaze returned to her. ''Not always,'' he answered.

They stared at each other, and Robyn's emotions felt murkier than ever. She tried not to let her gaze travel over him, but wasn't successful. She noted the way his khaki shirt fitted across his chest, the way his jeans conformed to the length of his legs. Then, quickly, she glanced upward, and was caught by the slate-gray of his eyes. Mark gave a slight frown, as if some disturbing thought had occurred to him.

''You shouldn't have come here alone,'' he said gruffly.

''I told you—I'm being careful. I came from the hospital with my uncle Greg. He and Aunt Janet are right next door. They run the Chocolate Shop.'' The Myers family had always been close-knit. Years ago, Cal Myers and his younger brother, Greg, had pooled their resources to buy this lovely courtyard of shops in the heart of Santa Fe, just far enough off the plaza to be ultrachic. The family enterprises included Cal's art gallery, as well as a store that sold hand-painted cards and one-of-a-kind gifts, another store that offered rare and antique books, and of course the Chocolate Shop, where delectable candy could be purchased. Each business did very well, and by now the Myers clan had a decades-long reputation for supplying excellence.

"I'm still concerned about you," Mark said.

"I can take care of myself," Robyn answered. But then, once more, she found herself unable to look away from Mark. Part of her said that he was the type of man you'd want protecting you. Another part warned that a woman might need protection against Mark himself. She sensed something unreachable in him—as if Mark Stewart might risk his life for you, but not his heart.

They gazed at each other, unsmiling. The moment might have gone on, but then someone pushed open the door to the gallery and a light female voice intruded.

"Robyn, I...oh. Excuse me. I didn't mean to interrupt!"

CHAPTER FOUR

ROBYN TURNED AWAY from Mark and surveyed the woman who'd just entered the gallery. At twenty-six, Emily Parkman, the young woman who managed the gift shop for Robyn's parents, was flat-out gorgeous, with large green eyes and unusual tawny streaks through her hair.

"I really didn't mean to interrupt," Emily said as she walked across the gallery, coming to stand practically between Mark and Robyn. "Two's company, and all that."

Robyn didn't answer. The truth was, Emily Parkman grated on her nerves. The woman was too full of herself—irritatingly poised, excessively confident. But, then again, maybe Emily couldn't help it. Her figure was statuesque in all the right places. Her skin was creamy, her hair gleamed. Everything about her seemed to shine. Every woman would love to look like Emily Parkman...and Emily Parkman knew it. Whenever Emily smiled, she seemed to be congratulating herself on her own good looks. Wearing that little smile now, she glanced from Mark to Robyn.

"Oh, dear. You really wish I hadn't barged in here, don't you? Not that I blame you." Now Emily gave Mark a frankly admiring gaze, and she spoke to him in a conspiratorial tone. "Robyn doesn't like me," she said. "She's only known me a few days, but already she's decided I'm far too outgoing."

Robyn stifled a groan. True, she had known Emily only a few days, but she'd had more than enough exposure to the woman. As if being knock-down gorgeous wasn't enough of an attention-getter, Emily would say the most outrageous things to make certain everyone knew she was in the room. Now Robyn studied Mark to see his reaction. But his expression remained impassive, and it was impossible to tell what he was thinking.

"Robyn, you *are* going to introduce us, aren't you?" Emily asked.

"Why not," Robyn said dryly. "Mark, this is Emily Parkman. She runs the gift shop next door for my parents. Emily, this is Mark Stewart. He's...a friend."

"A friend," she murmured. "Well...hello." She offered her hand to Mark as a gift, but he gave it only a brief shake. Emily seemed aware that she wasn't having the desired effect on him, and her manner changed subtly. She threw in a little innocence.

"I came over to see if you're going to reopen the gallery," she told Robyn in a well-meaning tone. "Your poor dad—maybe that's what he'd want, business to go on as usual."

"I was just checking on things," Robyn said. "I doubt my father's thinking about business right now."

"I suppose not." Emily addressed Mark again. "Robyn's parents have been great. They treat me like family. Nina has agreed to several of my ideas for the gift shop. She's even going to let me revamp the place. Nina trusts me. Robyn's the one with reservations." Emily gave another smile, showing how pleased she was with her insights.

Emily had been working at the gift shop less than six months, but already she acted as if she owned the place. And she was right—Robyn did have reservations.

Mark's expression still gave nothing away. "How many stores does your family have?" he asked Robyn.

"Only the ones along this courtyard—four altogether. Everyone in the family's carved out a niche. Dad handles the gallery, Uncle Greg and Aunt Janet make chocolates, Mom spends most of her time with the bookshop, and—"

"And I run the gift store," Emily finished. "A cozy little *family* operation." She gave Robyn the most patronizing of looks. "Well, I am supposed to be on the job. Give your mom a hug for me, Robyn, and tell your dad to hang in there. Mark...very nice meeting you." She gave him a dazzling smile this time, then went back out the door.

The gallery suddenly seemed quiet without Emily's presence. No doubt that was exactly what Emily wanted...to be remembered after she'd left the room.

Robyn studied Mark, but as usual it was impossible to tell what he was thinking. Had he been attracted to Emily? Robyn didn't like the niggling jealousy she felt. Lord, she was thirty-seven, and here she was envious of a girl in her twenties.

"My mother's delighted that she found Emily," Robyn said. "She was having trouble getting someone reliable to manage the gift shop. The two of them hit it off right away." Whenever Emily was around Nina, she took on the attitude of the grateful protégée, listening attentively to everything Nina said, offering her own suggestions in a respectful voice, seemingly anxious to gain approval.

Mark regarded Robyn thoughtfully. "You never wanted to run one of the family stores yourself?" he asked.

"As a child it was all I wanted. These four shops

seemed so magical to me—full of life and beautiful things, and full of people who cared for me. But my father always encouraged me to go out in the world and find my own niche.''

"So you became a teacher,'' he said.

"I don't remember telling you that—''

"Yesterday, in the coffee shop. You said you'd been feeling frustrated with your teaching career.''

"Do you always remember extraneous details?'' she asked.

"When they seem to matter,'' he answered.

She found herself gazing at him again. This time she made a special effort to glance away. "I imagine you're wanted back at the shooting range.''

"Benjamin pretty much lets me put in the time I want.''

"Everyone should have such an understanding friend, I'm sure. But I've told you, Mark—I'm being careful. You don't have to watch out for me, or whatever it is you're doing here.''

"Robyn,'' he said gravely, "whatever happened to your father isn't going to solve itself. Why don't you just accept my help?''

His offer was tempting. But she'd already let her father down on one promise. She'd refused to get a gun. Could she ignore his other plea? *Don't involve the police, Robyn, or something even worse could happen...*

"No, Mark. I can't," she said in a low voice.

MARK SAT on one of the benches at the plaza, doodling. The designs he'd made on the notepad appeared random, but he was thinking, sifting through what he knew so far about the Myers case. Of course, he'd read the police report, talked to the officers involved. He knew the basic facts. But it was the information he'd gleaned from Robyn that interested him most right now. Her family had obviously done very well in Santa Fe. Until a few days ago, the Myers clan had seemed to lead a charmed existence. Wealthy, successful—and, judging by Robyn, intensely loyal to their own. But now Robyn's father was in the hospital, which made you wonder about the charmed-existence bit.

Meanwhile, if Robyn kept turning down Mark's help, why didn't he just give up, forget about it? Okay, so he missed his job—missed it like hell— but that didn't give him the right to take over the Myers case. Besides, he had his kids to think about. He should be spending his time trying to rebuild his relationship with them. He gazed down at the notepad and drew some more random lines.

"Hello, Father. Busy as always."

Mark stood up and confronted his eldest daughter, Debbie. The perusal she gave him was cool and reserved.

"Thank you for coming to meet me," she said formally, as if he were the CEO of some important company who'd finally agreed to an interview.

"Debbie, you know I'm always glad when you phone." Something of an overstatement, since she hardly ever phoned.

"No one's called me Debbie in a very long while," she told him.

"Right...Debra." He remembered when she'd been happy to be "Debbie." She'd been an exuberant child, more fearless than Kerry. Over the years, she'd learned to focus her exuberance, concentrated her enthusiasm on achieving her goals. She'd won admittance to a private, very select college, graduated with honors and immediately landed a reporting job with an Albuquerque newspaper. The transformation had been complete then: adventurous, joyful Debbie had become intense, focused, ambitious Debra.

He motioned toward a wrought-iron bench. "Have a seat," he said. "Tell me what's new."

They sat down together, and Debra glanced around the plaza. "Nothing changes," she said. "Still too many tourists."

Mark glanced around the plaza, too. Sure, it was crowded, but his daughter didn't seem to see the grace notes he appreciated—the early-spring grass showing itself along the flagstones, the trees starting to bud, the ornate old lampposts, the weathered soldiers' monument rising in the center. A dog chased a Frisbee, a boy and girl walked with their arms wrapped tightly around each other.

Debra swiveled toward Mark. Now she stared at the notepad where he'd been doodling. "Nothing ever does change," she said. "You used to do that all the time, when I was growing up. You'd be working out your cases on a piece of paper. You'd crumple up one piece then start on another."

"You do the same thing," he said.

"No, I don't—"

"Sure you do. Ever since you were a kid...when you wanted to puzzle something out, you started drawing. Except that you were always a better artist than me. You drew animals and clouds, that type of thing."

"Really. How interesting. I use a computer most of the time now." She paused. "What's the case this time?" she said. "I thought you were still on leave."

"It's not really official," Mark answered. "Just someone who needs a little help...but won't admit it."

"You've always had a soft spot for 'someone who needs a little help,'" Debra said with the lightest of irony. Something about her demeanor suggested *she* would never be so foolish as to need his help. Mark felt it all over again—the sense of having failed both his daughters. He studied Debra, wishing somehow he could make things right with at least one of the girls. But how did you come to terms with a twenty-three-year-old who'd decided long ago she had no more use for her father?

"Anyway," Debra said, "this isn't a social call. Mom sent me to talk to you."

Something told him he wouldn't like hearing the rest of this. "Your mother knows she can phone me herself anytime—"

"She thought it might be better to have a sort of…arbitrator." Debra lifted her shoulders as if to express a neutral position. "She's ticked at you— she blames you for the fact that Kerry's scared about getting married."

Mark recalled his youngest daughter's tear-streaked face last night. And he remembered the exact words she'd used, her fear at ending up "unhappy and miserable and divorced." He swore a little under his breath.

"Debbie, the last thing I want is for either you or Kerry to feel bad about anything—"

"Well, Kerry definitely feels bad. It seems that last night she blew up at Frederick and told him he reminded her far too much of you."

Weren't daughters supposed to look for husbands just like their dads? Unless, of course, they were fed up with their dads. But there was another wrinkle to all this. Try as hard as he could, Mark didn't see any resemblance between himself and Frederick Graham.

"Maybe if I talked to her," he said. "Maybe I could find out what's really going on."

"I think she's made it pretty clear," Debra said. "She's scared to death of ending up like you and Mom."

"Okay," Mark acknowledged, "we didn't give her the best example. But your mother and Len have been happily married for quite a few years now. Doesn't that tell Kerry things can work out, after all?"

"Mom and Len *have* been a good example," Debra said. "They really care about each other, and they're proof that two people actually can get along. That's exactly what Mom's been trying to tell Kerry. But since last night, Kerry's been insisting she hasn't chosen a man like our stepfather. She says that instead, she's chosen a man like *you*. She won't explain to us exactly what the similarities are—she just gets upset and refuses to discuss it anymore."

"I'll talk to Kerry," Mark repeated. "I'll try to straighten this out."

Debra got a beleaguered look. "You really don't understand, do you? The reason Mom sent me...it was to ask you *not* to speak to Kerry. Not to get involved anymore. Just to leave it alone.''

''My own daughter's having problems—problems that are supposedly all my fault, and I'm supposed to bow out—''

''Mom thinks you'll only make things worse. Listen, maybe she's overreacting, but I think it would be wise for you to...keep a low profile. At least for now. At least until things settle down.''

''Keeping a low profile with my own family,'' he said, his voice heavy. ''That was the mistake I made all along, wasn't it? Not being there when you needed me. Sometimes things do change. I'm trying to change, anyway.''

''I'm sure you have good intentions,'' Debra said, her tone almost soothing now. It had come to this, his kid trying to placate him.

''The way it seems to me,'' he said, ''Kerry already had some doubts about this marriage—''

''Of course she's had doubts. She wouldn't be normal otherwise. Nobody goes into marriage without wondering what the heck they're getting themselves into.'' Debra's voice had sharpened. ''It's only when you're on the other end of things—when you can't even get a *proposal*—it's only then you think getting married would be the most marvelous thing in the world. Just shows how *stupid* you can be.'' Debra stopped this uncharacteristic outburst, as if already regretting it, but it was too late. Mark had a pretty good idea they were now talking about Debra herself...not her sister, Kerry.

"So," Mark said as casually as possible. "You still seeing that guy? Trevor, wasn't it?"

"Yes, I'm still seeing Trevor," Debra said, sounding very strained now.

"Debbie, tell me what's wrong—"

"*Will* you stop calling me that? And nothing's wrong! Except that my little sister's throwing away her chance to marry someone decent, and meanwhile, Trevor positively cringes every time *I* so much as mention a walk down the aisle." Debra scrambled to her feet, as if appalled by the words that had spilled out of her. She made an obvious effort to compose herself. "Forget I said anything, all right? Whatever's going on, I'll work it out."

His adventurous, ambitious Debbie...breaking her heart over the guy. Mark had never met Trevor, but already he didn't like him. He didn't like anybody who could bring that sudden look of misery to Debbie's face. Suddenly he wished both his daughters were kids again, nowhere near even thinking about things like marriage.

"Listen," he said. "Don't let this Trevor ruin your life—"

"Oh, stop." She looked truly miserable now. "You're only making it worse. Don't you see? You can't do Kerry any good right now—and not me, either. It's like we're both *cursed* somehow. Neither one of us knows how to make things right with a man. And you can't help. You just ought to leave both of us alone!'' And then, without even a goodbye, Debra went hurrying off across the plaza.

THE HOSPITAL had a walled garden where visitors and patients could go to find a semblance of normalcy. The flower beds had been recently tended, although no blooms had yet made their appearance. The daffodils were only now beginning to push their way out of the ground, too early perhaps; the weather had been unseasonably warm but frost was still a possibility. As Robyn followed her mother along the brick walkway of the garden, she felt sorry for the plum tree that had started to bud too optimistically. Snow could yet fall in the Sangre de Cristo Mountains, blanketing the town in winter once more.

Robyn glanced around warily, and saw a few other people strolling through the garden. There was nothing outwardly menacing, nothing that hinted at danger. She hated feeling like this, as if she had to look underneath the most benign of surfaces, searching for hidden threats.

Nina Myers sat down on one of the wooden benches, and waited until Robyn settled beside her.

"Isn't this lovely?" she asked. "I'll be glad when your father's well enough to take a walk with us here. It's such a peaceful atmosphere."

Robyn didn't think her father would be ready anytime soon for garden strolls. In addition to his physical injuries, he seemed emotionally broken. That hospital bed had become something of a refuge to him. Before this, Cal Myers had always embraced life, always surmounted with confidence whatever difficulties faced him. But it seemed he had now encountered difficulties he didn't know how to battle. If only he would tell Robyn the truth about the attack. Maybe then they could battle the problem together...

"I don't like leaving Dad," Robyn said.

"I don't either," Nina murmured. "But your aunt and uncle promised they'd sit with your father as long as we're away. Everything will be all right...you'll see." In the past day or so Nina had obviously been struggling to regain her old optimism. It seemed the only defense she knew: insisting determinedly that everything would be all right, trying to deny the worry and heartache that showed in her eyes. "We're all jumpy, dear," she said in a forced voice, "but I brought you down here on purpose so you could relax. And so you could tell me about the new man in your life."

"Mom, what on earth are you talking about—"

"Emily told me all about it," Nina said relentlessly. "How she saw you earlier today at the art gallery, with a very nice man. And how the two of you were gazing into each other's eyes."

"Mom!"

"It's true, isn't it? Why deny it? There's nothing wrong with having a boyfriend. It's exactly what you need."

"Mom," Robyn said. "Mark Stewart is not my...boyfriend. I've only just met him, and besides—how could I possibly think about a man at a time like this?"

"Your father doesn't want your life to come to a halt. He would be happy if he knew you were interested in someone."

Nina had it all wrong. *She* was the one who thought her daughter couldn't exist without a man. Cal Myers had always wanted Robyn to be independent.

"Mom," Robyn tried again. "Mark is just...an acquaintance. Why do you have to make it into something more than it is?"

"Emily was clear about it. She said you and this man were looking at each other quite fondly. It's true, of course, that Emily has romantic notions. I wish I could find someone for her."

Nina was the one with romantic notions. "Mom, I have the feeling that Emily Parkman is perfectly capable of finding a man on her own. She's not exactly shy.''

"Don't let Emily fool you,'' said Nina. "She puts on a lot of bravado, but underneath she wants the same thing all of us do. A real home, a family that's whole and happy.''

Nina refused to think anything but the best of Emily. Seeing the best in others…that was one of Nina's special talents. Although Robyn loved her for it, being on guard now and then wasn't such a bad idea.

"Mom—just don't let Emily make too many changes at the gift store. Business was pretty good before she came along, remember?''

"Yes, but at the same time business can always be improved. That's been the attitude in this family all along—we've never grown complacent.''

Robyn sighed. Yes, she knew all about the family search for excellence. That was why the shops had always done so well. But she doubted Emily Parkman could contribute any real improvements. Emily seemed more interested in advancing her own interests than anyone else's.

"You've switched the subject on me,'' Nina said. "We were talking about romantic involvements. Specifically, your own. Or lack thereof—''

"Some women like the thought of being unattached,'' Robyn said.

"Nonsense. Your father and I have been together for forty years, and I can't imagine any other type of life. You'd agree with me, if only you'd admit it."

Forty years of making a man the center of your life…that was what Nina had done. There was something poignant about it, but Robyn didn't know if she could ever do the same thing. Maybe one of the reasons she'd made such a botch of her own marriages was her fear that she'd become too much like her mother. The doting wife… Maybe, in reaction, Robyn had gone too far in the other direction. Maybe she hadn't doted enough.

She stood. "Let's get back up to Dad," she said.

A mysterious look came over Nina's face. "Wait, dear. We can't go yet. I've asked someone to meet us—someone who needs your help."

"Mom, what are you talking about—"

"Very well, I never could keep a secret." Nina rushed on. "It's Emily's brother. I did tell you that she has a brother, didn't I? Young Joshua. Only nine years old, and very much in need of someone who can tutor him. He's having trouble at school—and no wonder, considering everything he and Emily have been through. Both their parents gone, the two of them trying to struggle along as a family on their own. It hasn't been easy…but now we can help them. *You* can help, Robyn. You're a teacher."

Robyn listened to this flood of words with a dreadful sinking feeling. "Mom, I told you...I'm not at all sure about teaching anymore."

"That's just the point, isn't it?" Nina asked. "You need something that will help you realize how very much you *are* a teacher. So I asked Emily to drop Josh off here today. Why...here he is now."

Robyn turned around slowly, her apprehension about this situation deepening. She saw a young boy approach, scuffing his feet along the path. He wore jeans and running shoes and a well-used San Francisco Forty-Niners T-shirt. Robyn would have recognized him as Emily's kid brother right off—he had the same green eyes, the same distinctive features. He also had the same tawny hair, made unruly by a cowlick right in front. But this little boy seemed to have none of Emily's brazen assurance. He looked altogether too solemn, and he also looked ready to bolt at the first opportunity. He kept his eyes glued to the ground, but then, a moment later, he lifted his head, as if his curiosity had gotten the better of him. He gave Robyn a quick, searching look, just before ducking his head again.

CHAPTER FIVE

LATE THAT EVENING, Robyn stood inside the art gallery and flicked the switch to turn on her father's computer.

Then she glanced over at Mark Stewart.

"You're making me crazy," she said.

"All in a day's work," he answered.

Robyn sighed. "I keep telling you that I can't accept your help. That, in fact, it could be dangerous for me to accept your help. And you keep showing up anyway."

"What's that old saying about a bad penny always turning up again?"

She gave him a closer glance. The only light came from the track lighting in the front of the gallery, shadows deepening all around. In this atmosphere, Mark looked mysterious and forbidding, a man not easily reckoned with, the enigmatic expression in his eyes giving nothing away.

He had called her on the phone a short time ago, suggesting that she go through the art gallery's records to see if there was anything that might explain the attack on her father. It was a logical idea, one that she had considered herself. But she'd resisted it until now. It hadn't seemed right, invading her father's privacy.

"You were so damn persuasive on the phone," she said to Mark. "Pointing out that my father isn't being fair to me...that he's in trouble of some kind, but he won't tell me what really happened...so of course I'm justified in trying to find out everything I can. Believe me, it all makes sense, but I still feel rotten about doing this. And I feel rotten about letting you...a policeman...come over here—"

"Detective," he said imperturbably. "And I didn't give you much choice. It would be pretty foolish for you to do this by yourself, considering your father's warning that you could be in danger. Besides, it's not like my dance card's full."

Robyn frowned at him. "Mark, let's get this straight. Why are you really here? Is it just because you miss doing your job and this is the closest you can come to working on a case?"

Now he seemed uncomfortable. "Besides the obvious fact that you shouldn't be alone, there are two reasons I came. The first is, I don't like vacations...never been good at them. I sure as hell need something useful to do." He stopped.

"You said there were two reasons," she reminded him.

He looked at her. He still seemed ill at ease, but he said nothing. She flushed under his gaze.

"Mark," she began.

"Take it easy, Robyn. Maybe I'm attracted to you, but I'm not in the market for a relationship. I botched things with my ex-wife, not to mention my *two* daughters. I'm not looking to botch things with anybody else."

Now all Robyn could do was stare at him. He'd said he was attracted to her, but he'd made it sound like an inconvenience. Well, she certainly hadn't invited the man into her life. She hadn't asked him to feel anything about her, one way or the other. He didn't need to act as if *she* was putting *him* out, for goodness' sake.

"Look," she said, "it's not like I'm searching for a new relationship, either. My family's going through a crisis, and that's the only thing on my mind." She didn't know why she felt worked up. "Besides," she went on, perhaps more forcefully than necessary, "it's not just my family situation. There are plenty of *other* reasons I'm not looking for a relationship. If you want to know the truth, I have *two* ex-husbands. Talk about botching things—I'm the expert."

Mark's expression grew interested. "So you figure you win," he said. "Your two exes get you first prize."

"It's not a damn contest—" Robyn gave another exasperated sigh.

He seemed perfectly grave. "Maybe not. But I have to tell you the part about two ex-husbands, that's an icebreaker. Makes a person want to know more."

She sank onto a chair in front of the computer. "One ex-husband you can justify," she said. "Everybody's entitled to one romantic mistake. But two, it starts to get embarrassing. You're suspected of lacking fortitude, not to mention good judgment. You know the funny thing, though? My family's never blamed me. My mother's still certain there's a mate out there for me. And my dad... well, my dad keeps telling me that my marriages were learning experiences. At least, that's what he kept telling me before he landed in the hospital." At this moment, she longed for things to be the way they'd been before—both her parents' lives going along smoothly while *her* life was the only one in upheaval.

Dismayed, she felt tears smarting behind her eyelids. Any second now and she'd be bawling. The last thing she wanted was to lose control in front of Mark Stewart. She gave him another glance and noted the careful absence of emotion on his face. Maybe that was what they taught you when you joined the police force—don't sympathize too much with the crime victims, just work on the case until you solve it.

She willed her own emotions into submission. "Mark, you've seen that I'm safe and sound here. You can leave now. I'll keep all the doors and windows locked, and I'll call Uncle Greg to come pick me up when I'm finished. I'll be fine."

He sat down in a chair next to her. "Someone attacked your father here only a few nights ago," he said. "I'm staying."

Now he wore what she'd already come to identify as his implacable look. She knew she wouldn't be able to pry him out of that chair. And she had to admit one thing. She didn't really want to be alone, not here at her father's gallery, where the attack had happened.

She pulled her chair closer to the computer. "I'm going to do it," she muttered. "I hate being a spy, but I have to do something to find out the truth." She clicked the mouse to bring up the financial software. "When it comes right down to it, I'm spying on my mother as much as on my father. She does the bookkeeping for both the gallery and the bookstore, and she's taken to computers, big time. She's always up on the latest technical developments. Dad and I are the only ones besides her who know the password to get into these records." Her fingers paused on the keyboard.

"I won't look," Mark said.

"It's not that," Robyn said. "I just feel like such a *snoop*. Mom only told me the password in case of an emergency."

"Maybe this qualifies as one," Mark said.

Robyn felt the all-too-familiar chill seeping through her. Quickly she tapped out the password: Carmel. It was the place where Cal Myers had proposed to Nina more than forty years ago. Trust Nina to be able to combine romance and business.

Robyn pulled up the financial records for the current year, scanning debits and credits. Mark didn't talk. He didn't move, didn't give so much as a twitch. He must be really good at a stakeout, she thought. Ever-watchful during long hours. She made a genuine effort to forget he was here, tapping a key to bring up more information. For a little while she was almost successful as she concentrated on the task before her. But then...it was impossible. You just couldn't forget the presence of a man like Mark.

Her gaze strayed over to him. "So far I've learned that my parents throw even more business parties than I remembered. Art exhibits always call for a party, of course, and my folks have always known how to do it right. Best entertainment, best caterers in town."

Mark appeared thoughtful. "Any chance your

parents have been spending beyond their means, getting into financial trouble?''

''Not according to these figures. Mom always says to be lavish with the important stuff, then economize on what doesn't matter so much. It seems to work out.''

''According to those figures,'' Mark said.

''What are you implying?'' Robyn asked indignantly. ''That my dear sweet innocent mother has cooked the books, and we'll find her out?''

Mark didn't offer so much as a smile, and Robyn stared at him in frustration all over again. ''You act as if it's really a possibility,'' she told him. ''One of my parents capable of doing something illegal.''

''I didn't say anything,'' he remarked mildly.

''You don't have to say anything. It's your whole attitude. You seem like the kind of person who wouldn't be surprised to find out your own mother has been up to something nefarious.''

He shrugged. ''*Nefarious* isn't exactly a word I'd use. But, no, I guess nothing surprises me.''

Robyn propped her elbows on the desk and rubbed her temples. She still hadn't had a decent night's sleep since arriving in New Mexico. ''Maybe that worries me is that I'm becoming a cynic, too,'' she said. ''I met this little boy today…a nine-year-old who needs some tutoring. He doesn't seem too sure of himself, doesn't seem too sure about school, either. He could use a boost as much as any kid, I think. But that didn't make me want to agree to the job. Maybe I've stopped believing I can make a whole lot of difference in any child's life. What does that tell you about me?''

Mark settled back in his chair as if he surmising this would be a long story. Robyn frowned again.

"Okay, so I gave in anyway," she said. "I agreed to be his tutor. English, math and history, three times a week. And this is right after I called my principal in Denver and told him I needed at least a month off—time to be with my family, not a nine-year-old boy who's falling behind in his studies. Am I crazy, or what?''

Mark gave her a measuring look. "Maybe you figure he's worth the effort. Maybe you're a teacher, and you can't resist."

She shook her head. "Oh, sure, I used to think I was going to march into a classroom and inspire kids to change their lives. I was so convinced that being a teacher was my calling. But then..." She told herself not to make any more confessions to Mark. But she couldn't seem to stop herself. He sat there as if he really *was* on a stakeout, and he didn't have anything better to do than listen to her. So she talked.

"Everybody gets so damn apathetic. The students, the administrators...hell, too many of the teachers themselves. It just starts beating you down until you even wonder if *you* care anymore. Budget cuts, one after the other. Parents who don't seem to give a damn about their kids, much less their kids' education. You start losing faith. You wonder if you're trying as hard as you should. And that's when you wonder if maybe you should get out."

Mark seemed to be listening to every word she said, but he still didn't show any emotion. She stood restlessly.

"Anyway," she said, "as far as the nine-year-old who needs a tutor…his name is Josh, and he happens to be Emily's brother. It seems my mother has founded the Emily-and-Joshua-Parkman Improvement Society, all on her own. And now she wants me to jump on the bandwagon."

At last Mark shifted position, and Robyn saw him give a slight wince. "The conversation's that painful, is it?" she asked, trying for a light tone.

"Actually, it's my leg. They got the bullet out, but it did some damage. Nothing that a little time won't fix, though." He sounded matter-of-fact, as if he were recovering from some ordinary ailment.

"What happened?" she asked. "Who shot you?"

Once again his face took on that hard, unreadable mask. "It wasn't anybody you'd care to meet," he said. "Let's just say I finally managed to track down someone wanted on a murder charge from a couple of years back. My aim was better than his.''

Robyn shivered. ''You...killed him?''

''No,'' he said. ''I told you—my aim is good. I don't shoot to kill unless it's absolutely necessary.''

His words implied that if necessary, he *would* kill. What was it like, having a job where that was always a possibility, knowing you might be forced to take someone else's life? Perhaps it accounted for the aloneness she sensed in him.

''Mark,'' she said, dreading her own words. ''Have you ever had to...kill someone?''

He waited a few seconds before answering. ''Yes,'' he said, no emotion in his tone. ''Once. There was no other choice.''

She didn't want to hear any more. ''I hate it,'' she said fiercely. ''I hate that in a few short days my life has come to this. Wondering if *I'd* have what it takes to shoot someone. Wondering where the threat's going to come from. Talking about things like this, things I've never even thought about before—''

''Talking about them with a detective,'' Mark added. ''That gets to you, too, doesn't it?''

''Yes,'' she said. ''It does. I can't help it—my father begged me not to involve the police, but here you are. Off duty or not, you've made it very clear you're always a cop. You're so darn intense about it.''

"Exactly what my boss says." Mark's tone was wry. "He thinks I need a break for a little while…need to 'kick back' a little. I tend to disagree—being a detective is what I do. If there's one certainty in my life, it's my work." He spoke with what appeared to be an unshakable conviction. Robyn envied him that. Nothing in her own life seemed very certain at this moment.

She sat in front of the computer again. "Mark…oh, hell. Let's get on with it."

During the next hour or so, they went through all the computer records, and afterward examined the receipts and invoices that Nina kept neatly stacked in a metal box. But there was nothing out of the ordinary, nothing that didn't add up, nothing that hinted at the reason Cal Myers had been so brutally attacked.

Robyn finally pushed away a bundle of receipts. "This is useless," she said. "We don't even know what we're looking for."

"It was worth a try," Mark said. "And don't give up yet. Maybe there's still something hidden in these records, and we just have to figure out how to look for it."

"My family isn't the secretive type. We don't *hide* things—"

"Your father's obviously hiding something," Mark reminded her. "Whatever happened that night, right here in the gallery, he's not talking about it."

Her gaze strayed unwillingly around the gallery, and she imagined the violence that had taken place here so recently. Had there been one assailant, perhaps more? She didn't even know that much.

She pushed back her chair. "As long as we're at it, we should look at everything. Come with me." She led the way into a room at the very back of the gallery. Reaching up, she pulled the string that turned on the overhead light. "This is the official storage room," she said. "All the records from past years are kept in the boxes along that wall. And there are some other boxes that look positively ancient—who knows what's moldering away in those. Maybe we'll find something, after all." She tried to sound optimistic, and then the irony struck her: She was hoping to find something that would incriminate her father.

Before she could hesitate any longer, she began hauling one of the dusty old boxes into her arms. It was heavier than she'd bargained for, however, and she ended up swaying backward. Mark immediately put his arms around the box, anchoring the load. They were now standing very close together.

Robyn looked into his eyes and an unsettling ripple of awareness went through her. She clung to her end of the box, as if that would steady her against the bewildering sensations that had suddenly flared in her. Mark gazed back at her. His eyebrows came together, as if he was puzzling out a particularly vexing problem. He drew the box away from her, set it on the floor and turned back to her. They were still standing too close to each other. Robyn told herself to step away, but somehow she couldn't move. Mark continued to gaze at her with a slight frown. Then he bent his head and kissed her.

At first it was the lightest of kisses, Mark's lips scarcely brushing hers. Robyn was taken by surprise. She knew that all she had to do was step away from him. She knew that was what she ought to do. But she stayed where she was, her face tilted toward Mark. And then, ever so slowly, the kiss became something more. Mark deepened the contact between them. And, with the taste of his lips on hers, everything terrible that had happened these past few days seemed to recede. It was as if she suddenly found herself gliding over a beautiful lake, far from threatening shores. She felt a warmth spread through her. It seemed the most natural thing in the world to let him take her in his arms. She moved her hands inside the light baseball jacket he wore, seeking yet more closeness. Her fingers bumped against cool metal…the metal of a gun. Mark was carrying the thing in a shoulder holster.

All the terrible events came flooding right back. How had she allowed herself to forget? Her family needed her—needed all her attention and concern—and she was kissing Mark Stewart! She pulled away.

"Robyn," he said.

She made the mistake of gazing into his eyes. She saw the way they had darkened to a cinder gray.

A sound came from the main room of the gallery. It was a faint rustling, as if a breeze had quivered over the receipts and other papers left on the desk. But Robyn knew that all the windows in the gallery were shut, both doors locked tight. She'd checked them herself.

Already Mark had slipped his hand inside his jacket and brought out his gun. He inched his way from the storeroom, moving without making a single noise. Heart thudding, Robyn stayed close behind him. Stealthily they moved into the main gallery. Robyn drew in her breath when she saw the front door standing wide open to the night—the very door she had bolted so securely only a short time ago. She glanced around wildly, wondering who or what she would find. But no one else was here...all she saw was a few receipts that had drifted from the desk to the floor.

Mark gripped Robyn's arm. "Stay with me," he said in a low voice. He didn't have to ask twice—

she wasn't going anywhere on her own. Together they slipped out the door of the gallery and made a quick scan of the courtyard. Robyn strained to see through the darkness, all too well picturing someone lurking in the shrubbery or around a corner. But it didn't appear anything could take Mark unawares. He seemed to glance in all directions at once as he and Robyn went round the back of the shops. They made a full circuit, only to find no sign of anyone.

Inside the gallery once again, Mark thoroughly checked the main area, the washroom, the storage room, Robyn right at his side. She found her teeth beginning to chatter, and she had to speak.

"I'm—I'm glad you kept me with you. I've seen too many of those movies, you know, the ones where the hero tells the heroine to wait for him, and then he comes back and of course she's not there anymore..."

"It had to be someone who has a key to the gallery," Mark said, responding to queries of his own. "We should have heard the door being unlocked...of course, we were preoccupied at the time, at the back of the gallery, and whoever it was obviously decided to be careful. We didn't hear anything until he—or she—reached the desk. And then, to be able to leave again so quickly and silently...it was someone who knew exactly what he was doing.''

He...or she. Either way, Robyn hated the thought of someone invading the gallery with such silent, skillful intent.

"We were preoccupied, all right," she said grimly. "Way too preoccupied. Believe me, I'm the first to say we shouldn't have been doing what we were doing—"

"Who else has keys to the place, Robyn?" he said, ignoring her remark.

Trembling, she went to the front door, locked it again, checked the bolt twice. She checked the back door, too, even though she knew how useless the effort was. She could not rid herself of that eerie image: the door open wide to the night, those receipts scattered from the desk onto the floor. Now she bent to pick them up.

"Both my parents have a key," she said. "My aunt and uncle, too, of course. Everyone in the family has access to all the shops. No one else that I know of."

"Think, Robyn. Any friends of your parents who might have been given a key? Former employees?"

"I don't know. I suppose it's possible—"

"Does Emily Parkman have a key?"

Robyn wished he would stop grilling her, making

her feel vaguely guilty, as if somehow *she'd* been handing out keys left and right.

"Emily…I don't know," she said. "Mom might have asked her to keep an eye on things while the gallery's closed. But Emily doesn't seem the type to sneak around."

He made another quick tour of the gallery, his expression intent. There was a remoteness to him now, as if all that concerned him was the problem at hand.

A knock came at the front door, and Robyn almost jumped. Mark, still holding his gun at the ready, went toward the door and peered through the glass. Robyn followed close behind, peering out, too.

"It's Uncle Greg," she said, undoing the lock and swinging the door open. Mark slid his gun back inside his jacket, but still his watchful stance said he was ready for anything.

Greg Myers stepped over the threshold. "Are you all right?" he asked Robyn. "I was driving by when I saw the lights on, and thought I'd better check things out." He gave Mark a suspicious once-over, obviously ready to defend his niece. Since he and Aunt Janet didn't have any children of their own, he'd always looked out for Robyn as if she were his own daughter. Uncle Greg was a large, burly man.

Robyn had always marveled that a man with such big, sturdy fingers could make such delicate chocolates. And she'd always loved the delicious aroma that surrounded her uncle. While some men smelled of tobacco or aftershave, wherever Uncle Greg went he carried with him a whiff of chocolate, a hint of toffee. Unfortunately, Uncle Greg could no longer eat the very candy he made. After suffering a heart attack less than a year ago, he'd been under strict orders to change his diet and to stay away from stress.

"I'm fine," Robyn assured him now. "But apparently someone broke in here a few minutes ago—well, it wasn't exactly a break-in, since whoever it was used a key." She listened to herself, amazed that she could sound so conversational. "Anyway, Uncle Greg, this is Mark Stewart, a…friend of mine."

Mark didn't wait for any more social amenities.

"You just happened to be driving by?" he asked. Robyn wondered if he knew how to pose a question without making it sound like a police interrogation.

Uncle Greg ignored Mark. "What's this break-in you're talking about?" Her uncle had on his combative look. It was a family saying that in another lifetime, Greg would have pursued a career of military glory. In this lifetime, he'd contented himself by becoming an expert on military history; he could tell you anything and everything you wanted to know about the Napoleonic Wars. Robyn had many childhood memories of perching on a stool at the Chocolate Shop while Uncle Greg explained the Battle of Leipzig or Waterloo, marshaling candies into opposing armies.

"Are you sure you're all right?" he asked Robyn now.

"We didn't even see who did it, Uncle Greg. We were…back in the storeroom. When we came out, the front door was standing wide open." She waved the receipts she continued to hold in one hand. "Apparently whoever broke in was curious about these. The whole thing just gives me the creeps. And it doesn't make any sense. Whoever it was must have known we were in here—we had the lights on. So why did they pick this particular time to make an entrance?"

"Maybe someone wanted to make a statement," Mark said. "Maybe someone didn't want you to start feeling too safe, Robyn."

Now she felt a chill so deep inside she wondered if it would ever leave. "You're saying it was a message…"

"One I damn well don't like," Mark said. "First thing in the morning, you need to get the locks changed. I know someone who'll do a good job. Meanwhile, I'll call in a favor and get a patrol car over here to keep watch on the place. It could be that the intruder was looking for something specific...maybe something they don't want anyone else to find. If that's the case, we have to make sure we find it first."

"Just who are you, Mr. Stewart?" Greg asked. "You sound like a professional—"

"Robyn can explain as little or as much as she wants about me."

Robyn didn't want to explain anything at the moment, and she'd completely lost her taste for detective work. "I'm going home," she said. "I've had enough for one night."

Mark intervened. "I don't think you should be alone tonight. If this was some type of scare tactic, it means you could be in real danger."

"He's right," said Uncle Greg. "You'll stay with me and Janet again tonight. Of course, we'd planned on being with your mother at the hospital, but we can change that—"

"No need," said Mark. "I'll stay with Robyn."

"Just who are you Mr. Stewart?" Greg repeated. "What do you have to do with all this?"

"Enough," said Robyn. "I'm just going home."

"And I'm going with you," Mark said. "Some-

one has to make sure you're safe—and that's all
there is to it.''

Robyn just didn't have enough energy to argue.
She looked into Mark's eyes, something that was
always a mistake. As usual, she couldn't look away.
And this time his gaze told her she didn't have any
choice.

He would be her protector tonight.

CHAPTER SIX

STRETCHING LUXURIOUSLY, Robyn pressed her face deeper into the pillow. Wonderful, contented sleep…it was something you didn't appreciate until you'd been deprived of it for a few nights. She nestled up to the pillow. If only she could go on resting…

But then, with dawning wakefulness, everything came flooding back.

Robyn sat up in bed, fully awake now. She listened intently for a moment. She didn't hear anything from the rest of the house, but she knew Mark was still here. She could feel his presence, as surely as if he were standing in front of her. Last night, after the incident at the art gallery, he'd brought her here to her parents' house, and he'd commandeered the sofa for himself. Uncle Greg hadn't been too happy about the setup; he'd wanted to take charge of her himself. Robyn hadn't wanted *anyone* to take charge of her, but at the time she'd been too tired to argue, her nerves too jangled. She'd given in to Mark.

Now she felt herself tense all over again. She slid out of bed, went to the half-open door of her room and looked out. No sign of him. She grabbed some clothes and ducked into the bathroom. Several minutes later she emerged. Teeth brushed, hair combed, fully clothed in jeans and T-shirt she felt a little more in control of the situation.

She went out to the center patio—the *placita*—of her parents' home. Nearly a century ago this house had been a girls' school, and it retained the charm of its former years. A low-slung rectangle of a place, rooms that had once been dormitories and class-rooms all faced the patio garden. That was one of the most delightful things about this house—the gar-den flourishing in the inner courtyard, sunshine spill-ing down upon it. At its peak, it was always some-thing to behold: the grapevine twining over the trellis, the beds of tulips, phlox and daisies, the little pots brimming over with moss roses and petunias, the snowy white alyssum working its way into every cranny. Long ago, Robyn's mother had instituted a tradition. Whenever Robyn's birthday rolled around in May, Nina would plant something special to com-memorate the occasion. A patch of forget-me-not, perhaps, or a border of gentian. It was always a sur-prise, and as a child Robyn had delighted in running out to the garden first thing on a birthday morning, eager to see what she would find.

Usually these memories made her feel happy and loved, but now they only made her heart ache. The house was too empty without her parents.

Robyn went across thé *placita*. She paused in a doorway, looking in at her father's studio: the easel propped up with a canvas upon it, the clutter of oil paints, the bottle with brushes jutting out willy-nilly, the morning light streaming in at just the right angle. The place looked as if it was just waiting for Cal Myers to come in and take up one of those brushes. Robyn wrapped her arms tightly around her body.

She heard footsteps behind her on the patio tiles, and then Mark's voice. "Good morning," he said quietly.

She didn't turn to look at him. She just kept her arms wrapped around herself and stared into her father's studio.

"When I was a child," she said, "I wasn't supposed to go into this room. It was my father's private place, where he painted. But the forbidden drew me. One day, when I thought for sure no one could see, I sneaked in and got into my dad's things. I started finger-painting on a canvas, and I made the biggest mess. When my father came in and found me like that, I thought for sure he was going to chew me out something awful. Instead, he just looked at what I was doing, and after a minute he started dipping his fingers into the paints, too. We finished the canvas together.'' She willed the tears not to come, told herself she wasn't going to lose it in front of Mark Stewart. And, after a moment, she was able to go on, her voice steady.

"That's something I've never understood about my dad. For as long as I can remember, he's painted. He's an artist himself, you can see it, but he never exhibits his own work. Absolutely never. It all stays hidden away here. He's never explained why he promotes the careers of other artists...but not his own.''

Mark didn't answer.

"I guess there's a whole lot I don't know about my father,'' she said. "That's what scares me the most. He's shut himself off from me, and from my mother.''

At last Mark spoke. "I've had that feeling, too...with my daughters. The sense that I'm being shut out. It's not a good feeling.''

She was glad he didn't try to comfort her. From what she knew about him so far, Mark Stewart was not a man to give comfort freely.

Finally she turned around and faced him. In spite of the fact that he'd spent the night on the couch, he looked as alert as always. Perhaps his hair was a bit more untidy than usual. That and the stubble of beard showing along his jaw added to his virility. He'd taken off his baseball jacket, but the gun in its shoulder holster was still very much in evidence. Robyn wondered if he slept with the thing.

"Look, Mark," she said, "I appreciate that you stayed over last night. Really, I do. But I have Uncle Greg and Aunt Janet. I can stay with them whenever I need to. It's not necessary for you to stick around."

"So you keep telling me."

She took a deep breath. "After everything that happened last night…it's more important than ever for you *not* to be involved. Someone coming into the gallery like that, when the two of us were there—maybe it was a warning for me to stay away from the police. And there's the other thing, too. The…kiss." The word dangled awkwardly, but she could tell that Mark wasn't going to help her out. He stood there, waiting for her to go on.

"I've been thinking about it a lot," she said determinedly, "and I've figured out what happened. I was vulnerable last night. Hell, I've been vulnerable since this whole thing started. Anyway, last night…I was using you to escape. I was trying to blot everything out."

"That's funny," Mark said. "I thought we were just necking."

His attitude definitely wasn't helping.

"Look, Mark," she said again. "So I ended up kissing you. Not exactly a good idea, any way you look at it. I'm telling you that I made a mistake. I don't want it to happen again. I have a habit of getting too close to men under... well, under certain situations. I met my first husband soon after I moved away to college. I was excited to be on my own, but I was scared, too. And because of that, I started depending too much on Anthony. Before I knew it, we were married, and living not so happily ever after. As for Brad, my second husband... no need to go into that, I suppose. But it was another mistake."

Now he was getting a dissatisfied look. "Robyn, I didn't mean to kiss you, either... certainly didn't plan it. It was a mistake for me, too. I've already told you—I'm not in the market for anything."

"Well," she said. "We're in agreement. Neither one of us wants it to happen again."

"Seems that way."

They gazed at each other. Then, with an effort, Robyn turned from him and studied her mother's garden: forsythia almost ready to flame golden yellow, reddish leaves uncurling on the rosebushes. Spring, a time meant for joy and promise, not this swirling fear and confusion.

"Mark, as far as your getting involved any deeper in my family's problems—the answer is still no."

"I've arranged for a locksmith to meet us at your father's gallery." He spoke as if he hadn't even heard her. "And, after that intruder last night, your father has to start telling what he knows. I've already talked to Al Donovan, the detective handling your dad's case. I've told Al that your father knows more than he's saying, and that he needs to be questioned thoroughly.''

Robyn swiveled angrily toward Mark. "Dammit, I keep telling you what my father said. Involving the police further means something even worse could happen! You had no right to do this—"

"There isn't any choice. Not after what happened last night. But I informed Al of the circumstances. I told him to be very discreet. He's a good man. He'll know how to handle it.''

The anger inside Robyn churned all the more. Mark had taken charge as if this really *were* his investigation. She despised being so out of control. She hated everything that had happened these past few days...and yes, that meant she hated Mark Stewart's presence in her life.

"Dammit," she repeated under her breath. She had a lot more to say, but the doorbell rang just then. She went to answer it. Mark came with her, as if he couldn't let her do even this much on her own—answer the blasted bell.

She yanked open the door, and Aunt Janet stepped over the threshold. Janet was a petite woman who looked much younger than her fifty-eight years. The bright jewel tones she liked in clothes—turquoise, ruby, jade—contributed to this impression, as did the fact that only a few graying strands had woven into her strawberry-blond hair.

This morning Janet carried a shoe box in front of her. "The little guy under the lid is a sparrow," she said. "I was on the way over here, and found the poor thing sitting stunned in the middle of the road. He was probably flying too low and bounced off a car." She carried the box to the patio and set it down. Then she knelt beside it. "Can you hear anything?" she asked. "I think he's moving around."

Robyn knelt down, too. This was nothing out of the ordinary for her aunt. Janet was always rescuing disabled creatures—not just birds, but the occasional cat or dog, or even turtle.

"Listen," she said. "I can hear him starting to hop around in there—can't you?"

"Yes," Robyn said, smiling. "He sounds downright antsy."

Janet inched back the lid of the shoe box, and the little bird immediately poked his head out. Janet sat back. "Just you watch," she said. "He'll be fine...he'll fly away in a minute."

She removed the lid entirely and the bird flapped his wings. Very gently, Robyn's aunt tilted the box so he could hop out. And, indeed, a second or two later he flew into one of the rosebushes. From there he soared into the open sky, and over the roof of the house.

"That was an easy one," Janet pronounced. She stood, and now she gave her attention to Mark. "Mr. Stewart, isn't it? My husband told me all about what happened last night. I was going to come over right then, but he seemed to think you two might want to be alone."

"Aunt Janet," Robyn said firmly. "Mark is just...a friend." She was getting a bit weary of introducing him that way, but didn't know how else to do it. "In fact, Mark is leaving right now—aren't you, Mark?"

"If you'd like me to meet the locksmith on my own, that'll be fine," he said. "You can give me the keys and I'll head over to your father's gallery right now."

She'd almost forgotten about the locks. She wished she could argue with Mark, but changing the locks at the gallery was definitely a good idea.

"Very well," she said reluctantly. "We'll go there together. And *then* you'll be on your way."

Mark had a talent for remaining impassive. Meanwhile, Robyn became aware that her aunt was watching her a little too intently. Growing up, Robyn had felt as if she had two sets of parents—Greg and Janet, as well as Cal and Nina. At times she had objected to all the adult attention, but she'd also learned to appreciate it. Her aunt and uncle had very much wanted children of their own. It had been difficult for both of them when no babies appeared, and Robyn had provided at least some outlet for their parental yearnings.

"Anyway," Janet said, "I'm about to pick up your uncle at the shop, and we're headed over to the hospital. I thought you might need a ride, but it sounds like you'll be busy." Janet gave Mark a considering glance, as if still debating whether to trust him with her niece. At the same time, Robyn noticed the strain in Janet's expression, the lines of fatigue. It had been a difficult time for everyone in the family.

"Are you getting any rest at all?" Robyn asked. "You and Uncle Greg have been at the hospital almost as much as Mom."

"We're holding our own. Don't you worry." But then another shadow seemed to cross Janet's face. During the last year, Janet had often got that lost expression. Robyn knew why. Some eighteen months ago, her aunt and uncle had gone through troubles in their marriage. Uncle Greg had even moved out for a time, to his own apartment. After his heart attack, he'd moved back home—the health crisis had seemed to draw Greg and Janet together again. Neither she nor Uncle Greg spoke about what their problems had been, but the sadness lingered with Janet. Janet, who took such care with wounded creatures, now seemed to harbor a deep wound of her own. Robyn had to resist the urge to hug her aunt. She knew from experience that Janet preferred that no one acknowledge her unhappiness.

"I'll be on my own way," Janet said, and then she went back out the door.

NINE-YEAR-OLD Joshua Parkman sat at the desk in the Myers's family gift shop, his sneakers dangling just above the floor. A tuft of his hair stuck straight up in front, exactly like yesterday when Robyn first met him. He wore the Forty-Niners T-shirt again; it appeared to be a favorite. His expression unremittingly solemn, he glanced at Robyn now and then from the corner of his eye. Meanwhile, his sister, Emily, presided nearby, refusing to leave the two of them alone.

"Josh is bright," Emily said in a tone that implied any relative of *hers* would have to be enormously gifted. "I've helped him with his homework before, and I've seen how smart he is. All he has to do is apply himself a little more. He has a great deal of potential."

"The sooner we start then, the better," Robyn said, hoping Emily would get the hint. But Josh's sister stayed right where she was.

"I'll admit I wasn't convinced when Nina first

suggested this tutoring idea," Emily said loftily. "But if it'll give Josh more incentive—fine. Just be sure you give me your bill, Robyn. Charge me the going rate. Your mother seems to think I'm in need of charity, what with raising my little brother and all, but she's got it wrong. We do very well for ourselves." Emily paused dramatically, smoothing back some of her gorgeous tawny hair. "Our parents died," she went on. "An accident, three years ago. Their car was hit by a drunk driver. Sure, that was hard to take, but Josh and I have handled it."

Josh ducked his head as if he didn't want to hear any more. Emily gazed at him, and something in her expression altered. The look in her eyes was now unmistakably one of love and concern.

"Bad things happen sometimes," Emily said, as if to herself. "You deal with them, that's all."

"You try, anyway," Robyn said, thinking about her father.

Emily gave Robyn a shrewd glance. "I'm surprised you agreed to a tutoring job. I imagine you have enough to do. You're certainly keeping *busy* with Mr. Mark Stewart."

Robyn gritted her teeth at Emily's tone. The truth was, however, that she couldn't seem to get rid of Mark. This morning, after they'd met with the locksmith, Mark had pointed out that they needed to go through all the boxes in the gallery storeroom. That was something Robyn had planned to do her-self...but somehow she'd ended up doing it with Mark. It had been a frustrating endeavor. All they'd found were old business records, family scrapbooks and photo albums that Nina had compiled, news-paper clippings on several of Cal's artists who had made it big. Mark, as always, had looked for the underside. He'd wondered if it was possible that one of the artists had a grievance against Cal. And he'd also asked her to identify every single friend or ac-quaintance who showed up in family photographs. Could one of them have a grudge? Robyn had begun to wonder herself, despising the way she now had to distrust every person ever associated with the My-ers family.

Emily had drifted to the window and was gazing out. "Of course, I heard all about the excitement last night from your uncle Greg. Good thing you had your Mark around. My, my, there he is," she said, "still watching out for you after your little scare. How sweet."

Robyn ignored Emily's snippy tone. "What—Mark's *out* there?" she asked. She went to the win-dow. Sure enough, that was Mark Stewart's Land Cruiser parked at the curb, with Mark sitting inside. He hadn't told her he was going to keep tabs on her while she tutored Josh Parkman. He'd just gone ahead and done it. Didn't he think she could take care of herself for one minute? He appeared to be reading a book as he waited out there, but Robyn knew him well enough by now. She knew that no matter how absorbed he might seem, he'd be on the ready.

Robyn stayed at the window. Mark glanced up and across at her. He didn't seem surprised to see her there. He gave her a small, mocking salute with one hand then returned to his book. Robyn felt herself flushing, and Emily studied her with a knowing expression.

"He really is something, your Mr. Stewart. If I were you, I'd look for lots of excuses to have him protect me. I'd use whatever strategy I needed to keep him coming around."

"Strategies," Robyn echoed. "I may be a total failure with men, Emily, but I don't use 'strategies' to manipulate them."

Emily's expression turned oddly brittle. "It's better to manipulate than the other way around, isn't it? Besides, all you have to do is figure out what a man wants, and then provide it. After that, the rest is easy. Take your Mark Stewart, for example. I can tell he's into helping people. Protecting them. So it's simple. All you have to do is make sure you're someone who needs protecting."

"He's not 'my' Mark Stewart," Robyn said.

"And I don't want to manipulate him. I certainly haven't *asked* for his help—"

"Whatever you say," Emily remarked. She strolled off to attend to a customer who'd come in. Robyn still felt rankled, but she went to sit beside Josh. He continued to slouch in his chair, moving his feet back and forth, his face resolutely blank.

Robyn fished through her tote bag and took out a small paper sack from the Chocolate Shop. There were two candy bars inside, made from Uncle Greg's special recipe. She set one in front of Josh. His gaze flickered toward it, then returned to unblinking status.

Robyn took a bite from her own candy bar. "You're missing out on something good," she said.

He looked at the chocolate she'd placed in front of him, and a debate seemed to go on behind that young face.

The candy bar won. Josh reached for it and took an impressive-size bite. Then, apparently, he remembered his manners.

"Thanks," he said grudgingly.

"You're welcome. My aunt and uncle made these, you know. They're the best."

They ate their chocolate in what was almost companionable silence. After they finished, Robyn put a piece of paper in front of Josh, along with a pen.

"This is a writing exercise," she said. "So...why

don't you write down how you feel about school. You can be completely honest, because I'm your tutor, not one of your teachers.''

He regarded the piece of paper quizzically, as if it might reveal something to him. Robyn waited. At last Josh took the pen, scribbled a few words and pushed the sheet toward her. She picked it up. SCHOOL IS FOR NURDS, he'd written in big letters.

''Fair enough,'' she said. ''Articulate. To the point. Only one misspelling.'' She pushed the paper back toward him. ''But I think you could be a little bit more specific if you tried. What exactly don't you like about school?''

For a moment he poised the pen over the paper. But then he dropped it as if in defeat. He gazed at Robyn.

''I'm no good at school,'' he said. ''But someday I'm going to play football, so I figure it doesn't much matter.''

It was the most he'd said to her so far. ''Even football players have to study,'' she remarked.

''I don't think so.''

''Really, they do,'' Robyn said. ''When I was in college, I had a friend who was an all-American. But he was majoring in economics and he worked hard at that, too. He used to joke that he was studying economics so he could manage all the money he was going to make as a professional athlete.''

Josh didn't seem impressed. Robyn tried again. "Okay," she said. "I have a confession to make. I don't know a whole lot about football. Maybe you could explain the game to me. You know, like draw a diagram, and maybe tell me some of the rules.''

This time he took the sheet of paper and began drawing X's and O's on it with considerable concentration.

"This guy here, he's the quarterback,'' he said in the kindly tone of one dispensing knowledge to the less informed. "He calls all the plays. This guy's the tight end—he catches passes over the middle. These other guys are wideouts…''

Josh got so involved in describing the finer points of the sport, the hour seemed to fly past. At the end of it, Robyn had a very detailed diagram.

"This is great," she said. "Just what I need. You know how it is—you go to a game with somebody, and you hate to act like you don't know anything. It's kind of like school in a way. You want to feel like you know the rules, at least.''

"I guess," he said. "But I'd rather go to a football game.''

"You know what?" Robyn said. "You tutored me today, instead of the other way around. Next time maybe you can let me tutor you.''

"Maybe not," he said. He slid off the chair and went to his sister. "We're done," he said.

Emily put a hand on his shoulder. "That's fine, Josh. You can go outside now and play in the court-yard. Just don't wander off."

"I never do," he said.

"I know, I know," she said. "You're a model citizen, right?"

"Right." He grinned at her, and she smiled back. Then Josh went dashing out the door.

Emily turned to Robyn, and immediately reverted to her usual condescending self. "How clever," she said. "In between waiting on customers, I noticed what you were doing—getting Josh to talk about what interests him. But can you get him interested in his schoolwork? That's your job, after all."

Robyn didn't bother to answer, and Emily became defensive.

"Things have been hard on Josh, that's all, what with losing our parents. A boy as young as he is, it takes a long time to get over something like that."

Whenever Emily talked about her parents, her tone changed slightly—just enough to make Robyn take notice.

Robyn went to the window again and gazed out. She saw Josh kneeling down, digging in a patch of dirt with a stick. Mark had climbed out of the Land Cruiser and had bent to speak to the boy. The two of them seemed involved in a man-to-man conversation.

"Your Mr. Stewart is still out there, like a guardian angel," Emily said caustically.

Mark Stewart, an angel? Hardly. He was a man who'd made it clear he'd seen a little too much of the seamier aspects of life. But there he was, talking to a little boy and at the same time ready to protect Robyn.

The worst part was knowing that, deep down, she was actually starting to enjoy it…she was starting to enjoy Mark Stewart's presence.

CHAPTER SEVEN

TWO DAYS AFTER that mysterious intrusion at Cal Myers's gallery, Mark was still looking for answers. His search had finally led him to a hotel some blocks from the plaza. Standing in the empty lobby, he took note of the unwieldy leather armchairs, the dark moldings everywhere, the immense brass chandelier lurking above. The only other person there was the clerk, a fellow who presided over the registration desk with an air of boredom. He yawned as he studied the photograph Mark had handed him.

"Yeah, he looks familiar," said the clerk. "Guess he could have been in here."

"Think a little harder," Mark said. "When was he here? Who was he with?"

The clerk yawned again. "Nobody's memory is that good. I can't even remember what I ate for lunch three days ago. Can you?"

"Grilled salmon," Mark said. "Take a closer look."

The clerk propped his elbows on the desk and took a long hard look at the photograph. "Yeah," he said. "I'm pretty sure I did see this guy a couple of times...we're talking maybe a couple of months back. I remember because of the woman he was with."

"Can you describe her?" Mark asked.

"No—that's just it. She was wearing a hat and she kept her head turned away."

"Age? Hair color?"

The clerk sighed. "I'm trying to tell you. The only reason I remember her is because she was trying so hard to make sure I *didn't* see her. She kept her back turned, and she was cloaked inside this big coat she was wearing. It was almost a joke—she might as well have worn a sign—Conducting Illicit Affair."

Mark took the photo back, and tucked it into his pocket. "Thanks," he said. "You've been a big help."

"Gee, you've really made my day, too," the clerk said sarcastically.

Mark left the hotel and walked the short distance to the Santa Fe River. Not that it looked like much of a river here—only a glimmer of water along the sandy bed. It had been a dry winter for New Mexico.

Mark leaned against the railing that skirted the riverbank. Legend had it that this was the place where, a century and a half ago, wagons from Missouri had come to rest after completing their journey along the Santa Fe Trail. He tried to imagine the wagons creaking to a halt, mule and oxen teams jostling each other, the weary but excited travelers scrambling to the ground. But then all Mark could think about was the news he had to give Robyn. It seemed her father had been having an affair.

Mark didn't relish the thought of telling her. He almost regretted having found out as much as he had. He knew Robyn was at the hospital right now, visiting her dad. Her mother was with her, as well as her uncle. But Mark had to tell Robyn that maybe she really didn't know her father so well. Maybe he could get her alone for a few minutes.

"Mr. Stewart...sir," intruded a voice. "Thanks for agreeing to meet me here. It means a lot."

Mark turned his head and regarded Frederick Graham, his youngest daughter's fiancé. "Hello," he said without enthusiasm.

Frederick leaned an elbow against the railing. He looked younger than ever, in a spindly, undernourished way. He needed a couple of good meals, not a wedding ring.

"Mr. Stewart, I'll get right to the point. I asked you to meet me so we could talk about Kerry."

No big surprise there. "I'm listening," Mark said.

"Mr. Stewart, the upshot is...she's talking about calling off the wedding. She won't even discuss it with me. She'll only say that she's not ready. But then she gets this look like she's about to burst into tears, and she slams the door in my face. That's the worst part, knowing that after she closes the door she's going to start crying. I never knew a girl could cry so much.'' Frederick sounded puzzled, and maybe even miserable. Mark was almost starting to feel sorry for him. Most of all, though, he hated the thought of Kerry being miserable.

''Fred…Frederick,'' he said. ''Believe me, I wish I could do something to help—''

''Maybe you *can* do something,'' Frederick said. ''That's why I'm here. I want you to talk to her, Mr. Stewart. Find out exactly what's wrong. She won't talk to me, but you're her father. If she's going to talk to anyone, it'll be you.''

Mark shook his head. Frederick obviously had not been paying attention to the dynamics in the Stewart family. Amendment: the dynamics in what had *once* been a family.

''Look,'' Mark said, ''I'm not a favorite with Kerry. The last thing she'd do is confide in me. She barely takes my phone calls.'' He didn't like admitting as much, but he owed some honesty to this kid who loved his daughter. He was certain about that—Frederick Graham did love Kerry. Why else would he be desperate enough to turn to Kerry's father?

''You're probably relieved that she doesn't want

to marry me anymore," Frederick said with unexpected dourness. "You probably think it's the best thing that could happen."

"I think Kerry's too young to get married, that's all," Mark answered.

"No—you have something against me in particular. I'm not dumb, Mr. Stewart. Give me a little credit." Somehow, gangly Frederick Graham managed to look dignified all of a sudden.

"You don't have a job," Mark said, deciding it was time for some more honesty. "And Kerry wants to devote her life to poetry. You can see how maybe I'd be worried about the economics of your relationship."

"I'll get a job soon," Frederick said. "It's just a matter of time. But what good will it do me if she calls off the wedding? You have to talk to her, Mr. Stewart."

"Kid, you don't get it—"

"I'm not a kid," Frederick said. "And I do get it. The reason Kerry's scared of marriage has everything to do with you, Mr. Stewart. Not her mother, not her stepfather...you. So I've come right to the source. You're the only one who can figure out what's going on with her. Are you going to help me, or what?"

Mark thought it over. His older daughter had asked him specifically to stay out of his younger daughter's problems. Don't get involved, Debra had said. Maybe she was right.

Mark studied his daughter's fiancé. Frederick still looked way too young. But he had a determined set to his features, something that hinted at the man he would one day become. Maybe that was why Mark found himself giving a reluctant nod.

"I'll help," he said, even as he knew he would regret those words.

ROBYN SAT beside her father, reaching over to smooth his pillow. "You're getting better," she said. "You're healing. Even though you act like you've given up, you *are* getting better. Just imagine what would happen if you put a little effort into it."

Cal Myers gave her a look that could only be called bleak. It pierced Robyn.

"Dad, you have to remember how much you love the gallery," she persisted. "And your painting...don't forget about that. You're the one who taught *me* to find the passion in life. It breaks my heart to see you give up like this."

Her father's expression didn't change. "I'm tired, Robyn. I'm tired all the time."

"That's just it, Dad—you *have* given up. But you can't get back on your feet until you show a little fight."

"I'm carrying such a burden, Robyn. You don't

know... And why haven't you done it?'' he asked. ''Why haven't you tried to protect yourself and your mother? A gun, Robyn...it's the only way I can see.''

She debated how she could phrase her answer. *You see, Dad, instead of a gun, I've somehow ended up with an off-duty detective who thinks you should tell the truth. By the way, I happen to agree with him.*

''If I knew what I had to protect myself from,'' she said, ''it would make things a whole lot easier. Especially after what happened when I was at the gallery.'' Yesterday she'd told her father about the incident at the gallery. Cal had been more distraught than ever, yet he had confided nothing to Robyn.

''A gun,'' he repeated now, stubbornly.

Robyn battled her frustration. ''I know that detective—Mr. Donovan—came to talk to you again. You have to cooperate—''

''No police. I was told...no police. That's all you need to know.'' He moved his head almost frantically on the pillow, seeming to feel he'd already said too much. ''Your mother...I want her to be all right. I'm worried about her.''

''She's out in the waiting room with Uncle Greg. I've made sure that neither one of us is ever alone, Dad, just in case...'' In case of what? That question had stretched her nerves to the snapping point. She paused, wondering how much to tell her father about Mark.

"Dad, you have to trust me. Why can't you do that much?"

Her father's eyes held a look of despair. "It's gone too far, Robyn. If only I could turn back...do you know what it's like, wishing with all your heart that you could turn back? And knowing you can't, not ever again."

"Nothing is that bad," she whispered, clasping his hand. "Nothing."

"Yes. It is." His words evoked a terrible finality. Robyn tightened her fingers around his, as if she could pull him back from the darkness that seemed to be engulfing him. But just then Mark appeared in the doorway.

Mark, who had a way of taking over a room, didn't have to say anything, didn't even have to make an effort. Robyn let go of her father's hand and stood up.

"Dad, this is Mark Stewart...a friend."

He came into the room. "Mr. Myers," he said.

Cal regarded Mark with a suspicious expression. "Who are you?" he asked abruptly.

"Dad, I told you. His name is Mark Stewart, and he's a friend—"

"Robyn, what have you told him?" Cal asked,

his voice very quiet. "I want to know who this man is."

"I don't mean your daughter any harm, Mr. Myers," Mark said. "I'm just here to help. You keep saying your wife and daughter could be in danger. But unless you do everything possible to protect them—for instance, tell who's putting your family in jeopardy—you're responsible if anything happens."

Cal struggled to sit up, his bruised face turning red with anger. "You have no right to judge me. You don't know what the hell is going on. And I don't know who the hell you are—"

"Dad," Robyn intervened. "Mark's an off-duty detective."

"Dammit, Robyn! I told you not to involve the police."

"I didn't purposely involve Mark. You told me to get a gun. I was only following your wishes, and Mark happened to be the instructor at the shooting range."

"Lord, Lord," Cal said, sinking back on the pillow. "This isn't good. It's not the way things were supposed to happen. Nothing is the way it should be…"

"Dad, we're trying to help. Everybody's just trying to help."

"You need to cut the bull, Mr. Myers," Mark said, "and tell us what's really going on."

Cal turned his head away. Suddenly Robyn couldn't take anymore.

"Mark, this isn't working," she said decisively. "You're going to leave, and I'm going to...to get some damn coffee, and my mother's going to come in and sit with my father."

Mark gave Cal another look. "You're responsible," he repeated. "If you don't tell the police what's going on, you're making a big mistake." He turned and left the room.

Robyn left, too. She could feel herself shaking as she walked past the waiting area, but she didn't even glance at her mother or Uncle Greg. Instead, she kept walking until she reached the elevators. She punched the down button.

Mark, inevitably, was right beside her.

"I'm really furious at my father right now," she said in a low voice. "Except that I'm so tired of feeling this way. Angry at whoever attacked him, and angry at him for keeping everything locked up inside."

"Angry at me, too, I'd guess," Mark said.

The elevator doors slid open, and she stepped inside. Mark stepped in beside her. There were other people on the elevator, and Robyn didn't speak again until she was headed down the main corridor of the hospital.

"Yes," she told Mark. "I'm really ticked at you. Was it absolutely necessary to speak to my father that way?"

"Being kind about it hasn't gotten you very far, has it?" he countered. "Somebody has to make your father come to his senses."

She just kept walking down the corridor. And Mark kept pace beside her.

"Are you serious about the coffee?" he asked.

She took a deep breath. "Yes," she said. "That's exactly what I need. A major dose of caffeine."

Mark placed his hand at her elbow and guided her to the hospital cafeteria. He managed the tray line as adeptly as he managed everything else: in a matter of only a few moments, he and Robyn were seated at a table next to the window, with coffee and a doughnut apiece.

"Caffeine," Mark said, obviously trying for normalcy. "Growing up, caffeine was a dirty word in my house. Sugar, however, was another story." He picked up his doughnut.

It occurred to Robyn how little she knew about him. "What kind of childhood did you have, Mark?" she asked almost reluctantly. She was still mad at him, but right now she needed something to center on.

"Like I said—lots of sweets. In my family, dessert was an art form. A kid's heaven, actually. You could chart the week by our desserts. On Sunday nights it was banana splits, Monday you could count on fudge brownies."

"Seriously," she said.

"I *am* being serious. My mom and dad were very responsible people who always made sure we got to school on time, did our homework, did our chores. I guess they figured all of us needed a little outlet every day—something that wasn't quite so responsible. Enter the ice cream and chocolate syrup."

She was unwillingly intrigued by this glimpse into his past. "Sounds like you have brothers and sisters."

"One of each. And we all still have a sweet tooth—my mother and father included. It's too bad I grew up in Deming instead of Santa Fe. My family would have loved your uncle Greg's chocolate shop."

Somehow she couldn't avoid another question. "Mark…were your parents happily married?"

He appeared to give this considerable thought. "I always believed they were," he said at last. "They never argued, or if they did, they made sure my brother and sister and I never heard. So it came as a shock to me when I was about twenty, and found out my parents had once gone to a marriage counselor because they were thinking of splitting up. They're still together, though, and I guess that counts for a lot."

"I used to think that counted for a lot too…" She trailed off when she saw Mark's look of concern. "What's wrong, Mark?" she asked.

"Robyn…there's something I have to tell you. And it isn't pleasant."

She watched as he took a photograph out of his pocket and placed it in front of her. She recognized the photo right away. It had been taken a few years back, and showed her father in front of the art gallery. How carefree he looked, all his charm and vitality showing through. Robyn wondered if she would ever see him like that again.

"Mark, what are you doing with this picture?" she said indignantly. "I realize we were going through all those photos together—"

"I only borrowed the one. I needed it to do a little investigating."

"You could have asked for it. You didn't have to *lift* it, for crying out loud."

"Let's just say I borrowed it. I didn't want to bother you with the reasons unless it became absolutely necessary."

"I see. You wanted to protect me—is that it?" she asked. "Or maybe you just wanted to railroad in and handle this *case* all on your own. Do you always have to be such a damn policeman, Mark? If there was a good reason you needed this photograph, you should have told me, and then—''

He gave her an almost pitying look. ''You're not going to like what I have to say, but here goes. I started making inquiries about your father in some of the other stores near your family's. I was hoping I could find a witness who might have seen someone threatening your father—that type of thing. What I found instead was a shop owner who saw your father going into a hotel several times with a woman—a woman who wasn't your mother. That's when I decided a photograph would help me out.''

''My father—going into a hotel—''

''I showed the photo to the hotel clerk. He said he remembered your father coming in a few times with a woman, and paying for a room.''

Robyn tried to take in what he was saying. She tried to tell herself this wasn't happening. She wasn't sitting here with Mark Stewart and hearing that her father had betrayed her own mother.

''No,'' she said flatly. ''I don't believe it. This clerk of yours is mistaken.''

''It's possible,'' Mark said. ''A lot of people pass through the place.''

Somehow the fact that he didn't try to argue with her dismayed Robyn most of all. She picked up the photograph, held it closer as if she could learn a message from it. But all she saw was Cal Myers's engaging smile, his straightforward gaze into the camera. She could discern no dark shadows, no hidden life.

She dropped the photo onto the table. "No," she repeated, but her voice was less sure this time. "Even if he *was* at this hotel, there has to be some other explanation. The woman he was supposedly with—what about her? Who is she? My aunt Janet?"

If she'd hoped that Mark would acknowledge the humor, the absurdity of the whole situation, she was disappointed.

"Neither the clerk nor the storekeeper could identify her," Mark said. "It seems she was wearing a hat, and trying very hard not to be recognized. Could it have been Janet?"

"Don't be ridiculous. I was using the most farfetched example I could think of..." Her voice trailed off as she remembered something. "Oh, Lord," she said.

"What is it, Robyn?"

She didn't want any more of Mark's questions. She didn't want to have him watching her with that sympathetic but resolute expression—the expression that said no matter how much he sympathized, he would do his job and find out the truth.

"Dammit, Mark," she said. "Can't you let up, at least for now—"

"It will be easier if you tell me," he said.

In spite of her doubts, she found the words spilling out. "What I remembered just now, it can't possibly be relevant...but my father dated Aunt Janet, back when the two of them were pretty much teenagers. Janet wanted to be an artist at one time, so she signed up for a class. My father was one of the other students. The way she tells it, when she saw how good *he* was, she knew her own art didn't have a chance, and she decided she'd better find a different field of work. Anyway, they dated for a while. I don't know how serious they were about each other, but after they broke up, Janet started going out with Uncle Greg. She says that was when she found her true love, because nothing could compare to the way she felt about Greg. They got married when Janet was only eighteen. Of course that's right about when my father met my mother, and they got married, too...it's all just family history."

"What you're speculating," Mark said, "is that maybe there's still something between your aunt and your father."

Robyn felt angry again, and she welcomed the anger—it was a way to defend herself against all these wretched suspicions. "No, Mark. *You're* the one speculating." She stood. She couldn't be near him right now, not after what he had come to tell her today. "I have to do something, and I have to do it alone," she said. "Don't come with me. Please…just don't."

She walked out of the cafeteria, not looking back at him. And, for once, Mark didn't try to follow.

CHAPTER EIGHT

ONLY A FEW MOMENTS LATER, Robyn stepped off the elevator and walked back down the corridor to her father's hospital room. Her mother and Uncle Greg sat beside Cal Myers's bed, making obvious efforts to cheer him.

"Honey, you heard what the doctor said. They could discharge you as early as tomorrow," Nina was telling her husband. "I can't wait for you to come home so we can put all this behind us. Isn't that right, Greg? We'll just put it all behind us, and go on."

"Sure," said Greg in a reassuring tone. "All of us want things back to normal." He looked big and solid and comforting as he sat there. Cal, however, had a bleak expression.

"I shouldn't go home," he said. "It's not the best thing."

"Of course it is," Nina said. "All I want is to have you with me...back in our own house together, where we belong."

Robyn couldn't bear to listen to any more. She

took another step inside the room. "Mom, Uncle Greg," she said. "I'd like to talk to Dad alone, if you don't mind."

Nina glanced up. "Nonsense, dear. What do you want to say that we can't all hear?"

"I'd just like to have some time alone with Dad."

Nina seemed about to protest again, but Greg stood up. "Come on," he told his sister-in-law. "It's well past lunchtime and we're both hungry. Let's go to the cafeteria and see what we can find." He managed to shepherd Nina toward the door. As he passed Robyn, he gave her an encouraging glance. So many times Uncle Greg had been a second father to her, but she couldn't lean on him now. What came next she had to do entirely on her own.

She watched until both her uncle and mother were well down the corridor. Then she closed the door and went to stand beside her father's bed. The bruises on his face still looked mottled. He kept his face turned away. She tried to feel pity for him, but the emotion failed her.

"Dad," she said. "Please tell me the truth. Did you…are you having an affair?" She was surprised at how easily the question slipped out. She waited for him to convince her that it couldn't possibly be true. Instead, he turned his face slowly toward her, and she saw his expression: more sorrowful than she had ever known it.

"No," she whispered, still praying for a denial. But her father, it seemed, would not reassure her with lies.

"It's over," he said heavily.

"Who was she?"

"It doesn't matter, Robyn. It's over."

"Of course it matters," she burst out. "Dad, you have to tell me. This…this affair of yours, and the attack on you. Are they related somehow?"

He gazed at her with that sorrowful, defeated expression. "Promise me, Robyn," he said. "Promise that you won't tell your mother. She mustn't know. Dear God, she must never know."

ONCE AGAIN, Robyn and Josh sat at the desk in the gift shop. So far today, every tactic Robyn had tried had met with quiet but stubborn resistance. Josh had made it very clear that where school was concerned, he was not about to make any effort at all.

"Let's talk about the history of New Mexico. Tell me, Josh, what do you know about the Wild West?" Robyn opened another book.

"Wild West…that's just in the movies, and television. 'Bonanza,' 'Gunsmoke'…I've seen all those." He put a foot on his chair and fiddled with his shoelace.

"That stuff really happened," she said. "In New

Mexico there were cowboys—and cowgirls. And real outlaws like Billy the Kid.''

Josh stared at her. ''Come on. There's no such thing as cowgirls.''

''Sure there is—right here in New Mexico. Girls are just as good as boys at wrangling horses and rounding up cattle. This book tells all about it.''

Josh stared at the book she held.

''Maybe you're not interested in the Wild West,'' she said. She could tell from the expression in his eyes that he was dying to leaf through the book, but he was not about to give in.

''Well, I'll tell you what I'm going to do,'' she said. ''I'll leave the book here, on loan. You can look at it whenever you feel like it.''

He shrugged. ''I don't care.''

Robyn sat back. She suspected that Josh's resistance had to do with a lot more than school. Last night she'd questioned her mother for more background on Emily and Josh Parkman. But Nina herself knew only the few details Emily had shared: the senior Parkmans had died in a car crash three years before, and ever since Emily had done her very best to support both herself and her little brother. Meanwhile, Josh's school performance had gone from mediocre to deplorable.

Robyn wished she could think of the right thing to say to this little boy. Admittedly, however, her concentration wasn't what it should be. She had a hard time thinking of anything except her father's affair. The very word seemed impossible to relate to Cal Myers: *affair*. But he'd admitted it. He refused to say who the woman was, but he'd admitted that he'd been unfaithful to Robyn's mother. And then he'd asked Robyn never to tell Nina.

What a terrible burden—knowing something like this, and not having any idea what to do with the knowledge. Half the time Robyn wanted to blurt out the truth to her mother. The other half of the time, all she wanted was to keep her mother from ever finding out. Nina Myers had dedicated her entire life to her husband. Learning that he had betrayed her, could well destroy her. Robyn pressed a hand to her stomach. Just the thought of her father's betrayal sickened her. She needed to lash out at someone. Even though it was illogical, she resented Mark Stewart for being the one who'd discovered this wretched secret.

Mark had gone down to Albuquerque for the day, to see one of his daughters. Before he left, he'd made Robyn promise all over again that she would be careful—stay out of danger. He'd seemed reluctant to go. Mark Stewart, always the policeman: discovering secrets that could destroy her family, and at the same time trying to protect her. The irony didn't escape Robyn.

She thought about all these things as she watched Josh continue to fiddle with his shoelaces. "You know," she said, "you really are smart, Josh. Would it be so bad if you tried to prove it?"

The obstinate expression was well in place. "I don't need to prove anything."

"Maybe not. But it must really annoy you when all those other kids get good grades, and you know you're just as smart as they are."

Not a blink. Just then Nina came hurrying into the gift shop. She looked agitated.

"Robyn...Robyn, I need you to come with me at once!"

Robyn shoved her chair back. "Has something else happened—"

"Just come with me."

Emily turned from assisting a customer. "Nina, what's wrong? Can I do anything to help?"

"No, Emily. Just stay where you are. Tend to business." Nina disappeared out the door again. By the time Robyn caught up to her, she was already halfway across the courtyard.

"Mom, what on earth is the matter? I thought you were with Dad and Uncle Greg." Cal had been released from the hospital only yesterday. He'd seemed very reluctant to go home, and Robyn could guess the reason. Now that at least one person close to him knew about his affair, being with his family could only be discomforting. Of course, he might also be afraid that his attacker would put in another appearance. Robyn had certainly considered that possibility. Just as Mark had made *her* promise to keep safe, she'd exacted the same promises from her parents: they were to stay with Uncle Greg and Aunt Janet so they would not be alone.

"Your father is fine," Nina said in a wooden voice. "He finally got to sleep, and I started going through some of the mail that's been piling up. I found something…" Nina sank onto one of the small carved benches that adorned the courtyard as if her legs would not hold her upright anymore. Hands trembling, she opened her purse and brought out a folded sheet of paper.

"It's a statement from one of our savings accounts," she said. "It's an account that your father and I aren't supposed to touch. You see, we always called it our dream account. We opened it a long time ago and started putting away money for the trip we've always talked about taking. A trip to England and Spain, when things aren't quite so busy…just the two of us, spend weeks exploring, meandering…our own romantic adventure. That was what we talked about, anyway." Nina's hands tightened on the paper, crumpling it. "Apparently, though, your father has withdrawn all the money from the account. You can see for yourself, if you'd like."

Gently, Robyn extricated the statement from her mother's hands. She smoothed it out and saw that three withdrawals in the amount of five thousand dollars each had been made from the account in the past month or so.

"Your father is the only one besides me who has access to that account," Nina said. "So of course it has to be him. Fifteen thousand dollars…oh, it won't really hurt us financially. It represented a dream, that's all." Now her voice wavered. "Obviously he wanted to keep this a secret from me. He never handles our finances, so he probably forgot that a statement would come in the mail sooner or later. But why would he need this money? And *why* would he keep it a secret?"

Robyn put her arm around her mother, trying to think of the right thing to say. How could she tell her mother about her father's betrayal? How could she break her mother's heart? On the other hand, how could she *not* tell Nina? Wasn't it about time for the members of this family to stop hiding truths from each other?

Promise me, Robyn's father had begged. *Promise me you won't say anything to hurt your mother.*

Robyn simply tightened her arm around Nina, offering what wordless comfort she could, her heart aching even more than before.

MARK WAITED for his daughter outside Becker Hall on the university campus. The building looked the same as when he'd taken classes here himself, more than twenty years ago. It had been built in what was loosely known as the Pueblo style, multitiered with rounded edges everywhere, roof beams jutting out artistically. Sycamore trees still clustered around the building, cutting down on the sunlight that filtered inside; Mark knew from experience that when you took a class in there, you often felt as if you were floating sleepily in green shadows.

Nothing much had changed about the place. Mark scanned the university newspaper and saw that students were still upset about tuition hikes and that there was still a movie theater in the basement of the student union. He and Andrea had gone to that small theater on their first date, and they'd eloped not too long afterward. A whirlwind courtship, he supposed it could be called. Two college students who'd been young and foolish, and who hadn't had the sense to slow down and find out if they were really in love. Miraculously, both of them had managed to finish school, but the two babies had come quickly. Little by little after that, Mark and Andrea had grown apart.

Now Mark walked restlessly in front of the building. He was beginning to understand something. Maybe what scared his daughter Kerry was seeing the similarities between her courtship and that of her parents. After all, Kerry had met Frederick at school. They'd fallen in love quickly. Maybe Kerry thought those kinds of repetitions were bad luck. Certainly the last thing Mark wanted for his daughter was a repetition of her parents' disastrous marriage.

When it came right down to it, he blamed himself for the failure of his marriage. He was the one who'd gotten too wrapped up in his job, who'd spent more and more hours away from his family. Andrea had been left pretty much on her own, juggling work and efforts to make a home. But how did you make a home for a husband who wasn't around? And how did two children forgive a father who hadn't been there for them?

Students began trickling out of the building. Mark glanced at his watch; according to Frederick's time-table, Kerry would be emerging any minute from her computer-science class. Mark glanced at the faces passing by, yet he didn't really see them. He was thinking about fathers and daughters. Take Cal Myers and his daughter, Robyn, for instance. Cal had done something pretty unforgivable. He'd had an affair—betrayed his wife, destroyed his daughter's trust. But Robyn hadn't stopped loving him. She'd told Mark as much, only yesterday. She'd confessed that she wanted to hate her father, but she couldn't. Her loyalty—and her love—gave Mark new hope. If she could still love Cal, couldn't there be a chance for Mark and his own daughters? He'd never betrayed their mother. He'd simply made himself too absent from his family. A big enough sin, assuredly, but maybe one that could be forgiven.

"What are *you* doing here?" Kerry had come out of the building and now stood a few feet away from Mark.

"Hi," he said, trying to sound casual. "Thought I'd surprise you."

"It's a surprise, all right," Kerry said acidly. "How did you know to find me here?"

"Frederick."

Now another look went across her face. Uncertainty tinged with sadness. "I don't see what Frederick has to do with anything—"

"He thought maybe you and I should get together, have a talk."

Kerry started walking briskly toward the university mall. She didn't invite Mark to accompany her, but he did. Today his daughter wore designer jeans and a denim shirt, along with a *concha* belt of hammered silver circles. Mark wondered again how she planned to keep up her wardrobe on a poet's salary—make that a poet's *nonexistent* salary.

"So," Mark said as he walked beside his daughter. "Computer science. Sounds like an interesting subject. Computers…wave of the future, and all that."

Kerry stared straight ahead. "It's just a stupid requirement. I'm not all that interested in it. The only thing I use a computer for is my writing."

"You write poetry…on the computer?" Mark asked.

"Of course. You can't turn in scribbled pieces of paper to a poetry class, even though that might fit your stereotypical idea of a writer a *whole* lot better than somebody who uses a keyboard."

"Hey," said Mark. "I'm glad you know how to use a computer—"

"So I can go out and get some *boring* job typing for people? Is that why you're glad?"

Mark tried again. "If you got a job with computers, it wouldn't have to be boring. You could be a programmer, something like that."

"Oh, right," she said. "Anything, so long as I'm not a poet. Is that why you came all the way to Albuquerque, Father? To smear my choices all over again?"

Okay, so he hadn't said the right thing. But he wished his daughter wouldn't call him "Father" in that derogatory tone. Anything would have been better. Dad, Pop. He could have gone for either one of those.

"What do you say we call a truce?" he asked.

"Maybe we could spend a few minutes together...being relaxed. Enjoying each other's company. According to Frederick, you have a whole hour before your next class."

"Who does Frederick think he is, my social secretary? I haven't even seen him the last few days, but now he's arranging meetings behind my back. I wish both of you would just leave me alone!"

"Truce," Mark repeated. "For the next hour, anyway."

She didn't answer. They reached the mall, where a few kids on skateboards dodged among the students.

"Let's go sit by the duck pond," Mark said. "I haven't been there in a while."

At first he thought she would refuse, but she relented with a shrug. "I can give you half an hour," she said. "That should be long enough."

Mark led the way up the grassy slope surrounding the duck pond. Sunlight glimmered on the water. Mark didn't see any ducks, but he saw one of the cantankerous geese that were noisily demanding food from the students. There were sparrows, too, alighting wherever anyone was willing to scatter crumbs.

In spite of her expensive jeans, Kerry plopped onto the grass, swinging her backpack down beside her. Mark sat, too, although his leg protested as he settled on the grass.

Kerry brought her knees up and wrapped her arms around them. "What do you want to talk about?" she asked in a cool voice.

"About you and Frederick, I guess," he said.

"It really isn't any of your business, is it?"

"Frederick seems to think it is," Mark said.

"So you're telling me you wouldn't be here today if he hadn't suggested it. I mean, you wouldn't have come to see me just because...just because you *wanted* to see me." She seemed to be making a special effort not to look at him.

"Of course I would have come," he said too heartily.

"Knock it off. You wouldn't have come on your own."

He couldn't deny it. He was tired of being snubbed by his daughters so these days he didn't try as much as he should. He didn't make the extra effort to get past the rebuffs and the rejections.

"Kerry," he said. "When you and Debbie were kids, all I wanted was to keep the two of you from being tainted by the type of things I dealt with on the job. I tried to distance you from my career—but in the end I distanced you from myself."

"Sounds good," she said. "But aren't you just making excuses?"

"I don't think so. Maybe I cared about my job too much, and maybe I was always looking for a way to get more immersed in it. But I also cared about you and your sister—"

"You don't need to tell me any of this," she said stiffly. "Haven't we been over it before?"

"When your mom and I divorced, it shook me up to realize how far apart you and I and Debbie had already grown. I told myself I couldn't let it get any worse. I tried—" No, this wasn't a good tack, either. Right after the divorce, his ex-wife had done everything she could to minimize his contact with his daughters. Andrea had been understandably hurt and resentful, and she'd taken it out by trying to turn the girls against him. Mark wouldn't bring that up with Kerry, though. No matter Andrea's mistakes, his own were far worse.

Now he watched as a sparrow hopped near. It reminded him of the bird Robyn's aunt had rescued the other day. The Myers family...a lot of love going on there, but a whole lot of problems, too. Did any family ever get it right?

Kerry opened her backpack and took out a sandwich. She tore off a piece of crust and set it on the grass. The sparrow pecked at it, and then another sparrow landed almost on top of the bread. A brief scuffle ensued.

"Kerry," Mark tried again. "Maybe the reason

we can't move on is that you never tell me how you feel. Sure, you make it pretty obvious that you're disgusted with me, but you don't let it out, not in so many words.''

At last she gazed at him, her face solemn. ''You want me to tell you exactly how I feel—okay, I can do that. It's easy. When I was growing up, all I ever wanted was for you to be with me. I mean *really* be with me. Really pay attention to what I was saying or doing. But whenever I was lucky enough to get you in the same room with me…you weren't there. Not really. Your mind was always somewhere else.''

''I'm sorry—''

''I could forget about all that,'' she said, not letting him finish. ''I could forget about what happened years ago. I don't like carrying a grudge. But you're still doing it. Even today—even right now—you're doing it. You're off somewhere else. You're not *here*, with me. I came out of my class, and supposedly you were waiting for me, but you were just looking off into the distance. And I could tell, before you'd even spoken a word, that you didn't actually want to be here. You were only going through the motions. Just like always.'' Her voice shook a little. She zipped up her backpack and scrambled to her feet, sparrows scattering as she moved. When she glanced down at Mark, she wore the disdainful mask that she seemed to have perfected just for him.

"At least you're not bothering to deny it," she said. "But you know what's really funny? Frederick is exactly like you that way. He'll seem to want to be with me, but then he's not really *there*. He'll just stare off into the distance, too, like he's completely forgotten about me. Well, you know what? I don't want that in a father. And I sure as hell don't want it in a husband. I'm not asking for every single minute of somebody's attention. Just a little bit of focus, that's all. Is it so bad, wanting that?"

"No," he said. "It's not so bad." Ironically she'd accused him of being distracted today, yet the whole time he'd been thinking about his daughters and how to get closer to them. He didn't think Kerry would believe that. She was too used to his failings in the past to give him any credit now.

CHAPTER NINE

ROBYN GLANCED AROUND the living room of Mark's apartment, asking herself for the tenth time why she'd given in and come here tonight. Sure, she'd had one hell of a day, but now it was late and the last thing she needed was the company of Mark Stewart, off-duty detective. Yet he'd called her on the phone, and now here she was.

"How was Albuquerque?" she asked, trying for a conversational tone.

Mark was in the small kitchen, rummaging for drinks.

His voice came muffled from behind the refrigerator door. "My daughter despises the very sight of me."

So maybe he'd had a hell of a day, too. "I'm sorry," Robyn said.

He shut the refrigerator door and emerged with a couple of cans of beer. "Not exactly champagne at the Ritz," he said, handing her a beer and indicating the surroundings.

Robyn accepted the beer and evaluated his apartment one more time. The architectural details were pleasing enough: high ceilings, arched doorways, the kind of old-fashioned phone nook one rarely saw anymore. The 1940s atmosphere was pervasive, and Robyn liked it. However, Mark's decor left a lot to be desired. No paintings on the walls, a futon frame with no mattress or cushions, and floors with no rugs. The place was characterized most of all by the absence of things.

"This place looks barely lived in," she said. "How long have you been here, anyway?"

"About six months," he said. "I just can't seem to find the right place."

Robyn sat down in the one armchair, a surprisingly comfortable item, and Mark set up a folding chair for himself. Turning it around, he sat so that he could prop his arms along the back of it, and then he studied Robyn.

"So," he said. "Tell me what happened."

When he'd called her a short time ago, she hadn't been very coherent over the phone. She'd informed him only that the Myers clan had suffered an unprecedented blowup, and then she'd all too readily accepted his invitation to get away.

"Let's not talk about it," she said. "For a few minutes, at least, let's pretend the crisis in my family hasn't gone from bad to worse."

Mark sipped his beer and went on studying her.

She found herself gazing back at him…at his soft dark hair, his gray eyes, the strong line of his jaw. Then she found her gaze lingering on his mouth, and she remembered the touch of his lips.

Maybe it wasn't such a good idea to try forgetting her family problems, after all. Robyn sipped her beer, and then she spoke quickly.

"Here's how it went. Today my mother told me that my father has cleaned out one of their savings accounts…Without informing her, he withdrew fifteen thousand dollars that was supposed to be for a dream vacation of theirs. She was understandably hurt. It wasn't the money—it was that he would tamper with their dream. Anyway, after she told me, we went to confront my father. She broke down and started crying. But then…she started yelling. That was the real shocker—my mother yelling at my father."

Mark didn't look surprised by this turn of events. He just wore what Robyn had come to term his "waiting" expression.

"So anyway," Robyn said. "My dad blew up, too. He said it wasn't any of my mother's business why he'd withdrawn the money. He said she just ought to trust him. And she said how could she trust him if he was going to do something behind her back. Since they were both getting pretty worked up, Uncle Greg and Aunt Janet couldn't help overhearing—we're staying at their house, after all. Aunt Janet tried to be a sort of mediator, but then she ended up getting ticked at my father, too. She said that lying was the most despicable thing in a marriage. And Uncle Greg didn't say a thing, just stood there looking terribly sad... Oh, the whole thing was a mess.'' Robyn paused for breath, and meanwhile Mark took another swallow of beer.

Robyn stood and walked restlessly to the other end of the living room. Her heels made a hollow clicking sound on the bare wooden floor. ''I don't think I've left anything out,'' she said, ''except that Aunt Janet finally left the room as if she couldn't take any more. I followed her... I asked her if her anger was covering up any other emotions toward my father. After all, they'd dated all those years ago. It wasn't an easy subject to bring up, but I had to do it. Janet gave me a stricken look and said old feelings for my father were positively the last thing on her mind. Maybe she was thinking about Uncle Greg and the problems they'd had in their own marriage...I don't know, but I guess that covers just about everything. The Myers family, coming apart at the seams.''

Mark set down his beer. ''The part about your father cleaning out the savings account, let's start there.''

''No, Mark. Let's not start anywhere. I already

told you what happened. Now I just want…I just want to forget about everything. My father's affair, and all the rest of it.''

He stood and came over next to her. ''I'm sorry,'' he said simply.

She gazed at him, and she could think of one way to forget. If Mark would take her into his arms, and kiss her again…

How could she be so weak? But she felt as if she'd been standing in the cold for a very long while, and now the promise of warmth was before her. She felt herself tremble, and Mark hadn't even touched her.

He frowned a little, seeming to question why he'd come to her. But then he lifted his hand and ran a finger ever so lightly across her lips. It was only the briefest touch, but the warmth went through her. And yes…she needed more. She was the one who took a step closer to Mark. And she was the one who lifted her face to his.

The kiss was inevitable. Mark framed her face with both his hands, brought her closer to him. At first his lips were gentle upon hers, but then gradually became more insistent. She responded eagerly, taking what she needed from him, what she craved. But the hunger would not be satiated. Instead, it flared into a deeper longing.

At last some shred of will allowed her to pull

away. "No, Mark," she said, her voice shaking. "We can't do this." She moved away, seeking to put a safe distance between them. It didn't help; she felt as if he had left an imprint of warmth upon her, and she wanted more. "I know what's happening," she said. "It's like I told you...when I'm feeling vulnerable, I tend to lean on a man. It's a bad habit, and I have to stop giving in to it."

Mark ran a hand through his hair. "So this is about your ex-husbands," he said.

"In a way, yes." It seemed important to explain. "My first ex and I had been divorced for a couple of years when he showed up in my life again. He convinced me how much things had changed...how much *he* had changed. So we began seeing each other again...even discussed the possibility of re-marrying. Only he ended up walking out on me all over again. That was a low point for me—very low. I was ashamed and embarrassed, and that made me way too susceptible. So that was when I met husband number two and married *him*. Let me give you a clue, Mark. Never marry anybody when you're on the rebound. Chances are, you'll soon have another ex."

"Are you on the rebound now?" he asked.

She began pacing again. "I don't know—yes. Maybe. Divorce number two became final only five months ago. And now, all this with my family...it would be so easy for me to lean on someone, my judgment is probably off." She knew what she ought to do now. She ought to walk out the door and go back to her uncle and aunt's house, no matter how much she wished to stay right here.

"Robyn, I've already told you I'm not looking for anything more in my own life. I'm no good at relationships."

Something in his tone put her on the defensive. "Believe me, Mark, I'm not envisioning a relationship, either."

"What do you want, Robyn?" His voice was very matter-of-fact. She looked at him, and somehow knew she had to be completely honest.

"Dammit, Mark...I want you to hold me. I want you to kiss me...and yes, I want you to make love to me. But I know it's wrong. I know we have absolutely no foundation for such a thing. We've met under all the wrong circumstances. And when I look at you, Mark...all I have are questions. Am I just trying to escape everything that's happened in my family? Am I just looking for solace, for comfort? And how can any of that be a good reason for making love?"

"I don't know," Mark said. "I don't have the answers. And hell, I've got enough problems without adding anything else to the mix. But that doesn't change one thing, Robyn. I want you, too."

They stood apart, just looking at each other. Robyn prayed for the strength to turn from him and walk out the door before it was too late. Her prayer went unanswered. Instead, she stayed put, yearning for the forbidden, watching how his eyes darkened, how his muscles tensed.

This time she didn't know which one of them made the first move. It didn't really matter, because she was once again lost in his embrace. All her arguments had done no good. All she had was this...the longing that flamed inside her, refusing to be denied. She clung to Mark, twining her fingers in his hair, molding her body to his. His arms tightened around her.

The kiss might have lasted one minute, or several. Robyn lost track of everything but the heat of Mark's touch. And when at last they separated for breath, there was a question deep in his eyes. They gazed at each other for what seemed a very long while. The question remained in Mark's eyes, and at last Robyn gave the slightest of nods.

She held on to him as he guided her down a short hallway and across the threshold of another room. A glimmer of lamplight from the living room managed to reach here, enough for her to see that the main piece of furniture was a bed, its sheets and blanket rumpled. Mark paused inside the doorway, as if to give Robyn time to change her mind. Maybe he didn't realize that she'd gone way past the point where she could change anything about this night. And so it was she who took the final few steps to the bed.

Together they sank down upon the mattress. Robyn brought her arms around Mark. He bent his head and kissed her throat. Then he caressed her, his touch achingly warm even through the cloth of her blouse. Only little by little did each caress become more bold, more provocative…Mark's hand ever so light upon her hip, her own traveling over his chest…

Finally she tugged at the buttons of his shirt. The need inside her was flaring, demanding yet more fulfillment, carrying her yet further away. Impatient, she managed to get his shirt open. She moved her fingers over the swirl of hair that tapered down toward his jeans. Now he fumbled with her buttons, and with the zipper of her skirt. She arched upward, trying to help him. He gave the slightest of groans. When he spoke, his voice was husky with desire, but she detected something else as well.

"Just my leg," he said. "The damn wound. Forget about it…" Together they slipped off her skirt, her blouse. Mark pushed up the flimsy material of her camisole and trailed his lips over her skin. She gasped with the response that went through her body, the heat gathering deep inside her.

"Mark…"

With both hands, he eased her panties away from her hips. She arched toward him again. She'd never known this sense of abandon with anyone, never known such recklessness. He lifted himself over her, and she heard the acceleration in his breath. "Robyn…" His voice was strained. "I probably have something around here somewhere…a condom…"

She didn't want to stop, but at least some remnant of common sense made her still her hands on his chest. He got up and went to search through a bureau drawer…then another one. At last he found a condom, and came back to her. A moment or two later he began to caress her again.

He took it slowly this time, every touch a deliberate prolonging of sensation. Robyn followed where he led, a captive to each kiss, each gentle tantalizing stroke. It seemed that every part of her came alive to Mark, in ways she'd never known before. He awoke in her feelings almost too keen, too intense to bear. And so Robyn opened herself to Mark, drew him into her with a yearning that made her gasp again. Now it was she who incited with her touch, her own caresses urging him to hold nothing back.

They moved in a rhythm they found together. At last Robyn cried out with the exquisite intensity that burst inside her. And then Mark added his own sounds to hers, as if the sensations between them could not possibly be contained in silence.

The silence descended afterward, when Robyn slowly came back to reality and realized what an absurd position she was in. She lay tangled with Mark, her undies dangling from one foot, her camisole twisted up around her neck. It was the position of someone who had thoroughly indulged in every aspect of sex. Oh, yes, she'd managed to escape her problems—but only for a few impetuous moments. Now everything came rushing back, this time accompanied by dismay.

She separated herself from Mark, but she could feel the dampness of his sweat on her skin—another imprint he had left upon her. "Oh, no," she said.

He lifted onto one elbow. "I was thinking more along the lines of 'oh, yes.'"

She yanked her camisole back in place, pulled up her panties. Then she began searching almost frantically for her skirt and blouse. "This was a mistake, Mark. We both knew it from the start."

"I didn't know this was going to happen tonight," he said, his voice completely serious now. "I didn't count on it, didn't plan it. But, Robyn...even if it was a mistake, we can't pretend it didn't happen."

"I wish I could pretend," she said, her voice low. "I wish I could pretend so many things hadn't happened." At last she found her skirt and slipped it on. After that she fumbled with the buttons of her blouse, and finally she was fully clothed.

Yet she still felt more vulnerable than when she had lain in Mark Stewart's arms.

ONLY A SHORT WHILE LATER, Mark drove Robyn toward her aunt and uncle's house. It was well past midnight, and he'd turned on the heater in the Land Cruiser. Warm air drifted over her. It should have felt cozy and comforting. Instead, all Robyn knew was that aching emptiness, and a coldness inside her that no amount of heat could dissipate.

The silence between her and Mark now seemed impossible to bridge, yet she found herself speaking.

"You don't have any pictures of your daughters," she said.

"What...?" His voice sounded distracted, remote.

"In your apartment," she said. "You don't have any photographs of your daughters around." She didn't know why she was talking about this. Any minute, Mark would probably tell her to mind her own business.

After a pause, though, he spoke. "I have pictures of Debra and Kerry when they were kids. But after the divorce, I wasn't exactly around for family-photo shoots." He paused again. "Maybe I'd display the pictures I do have, except that…"

He didn't need to finish the sentence. Robyn could fill in the blanks pretty well herself. Looking at photos every day would only remind him of the distance between himself and his daughters. And so his apartment remained bare, carefully lacking signs of a personal life. Why had she brought up the subject? Maybe as a reminder that neither she nor Mark was any good at a personal life.

They traveled in silence for another moment or two, and now their route took them past the Myers's family shops. Robyn glanced out her window. All the stores were darkened, locked down for the night…save one. Light blazed from the gift shop, and the front door was wide open. Nothing could have been more abnormal at this time of night.

"Stop!" Robyn exclaimed. Her instruction wasn't necessary, for Mark had already wheeled into the parking lot. The Land Cruiser came to a jolting halt.

"Stay here," Mark said as he opened his door. Robyn didn't need to look to know that he'd reached inside his coat and pulled out his gun. But she ignored his command, sliding out her own side of the vehicle and staying right beside him as he moved toward the gift shop. She stared at that gaping door, remembering the night when someone had intruded

on the art gallery. There had been a door open that
time, too, flung wide to the darkness.

Robyn found herself latching on to Mark's coat.
He reached the threshold of the shop, as always
moving with skillful alertness. Robyn reassured herself that nothing too awful could happen with Mark
always at the ready—

"Don't look," he said suddenly, turning to block
her view. But it was already too late. Robyn had
stepped over the threshold, and she saw Emily...gorgeous young Emily Parkman, lying on the
floor in a pool of blood. Lovely Emily, her eyes
open wide in an expression almost of bemusement.
Emily, who almost seemed to have been smiling
when she died.

DETECTIVE TOM GRANGER was thorough at his job.
Right now he was making certain that every detail
was attended to—photographs taken, fingerprints
lifted, notes and reports carefully written. And Tom
did all this while wearing a well turned-out suit in
pinstripes. As far as Mark was concerned, there was
something unnatural about a jacket and a pair of
pants that matched to perfection. Mark himself had
never been partial to suits.

Tom strolled across the gift shop toward Mark,
adeptly skirting Emily Parkman's body as he came.
"Well, Stewart," he said. "Imagine you being the

closest thing we've got to a witness. All we know so far is that she was shot at medium range, .38-caliber most likely." Then, as if to assert his authority, he added, "We'll get it nailed down. Meanwhile, you can get on with your vacation."

Mark and Tom had known each other long enough for Tom to be perfectly aware just how much the term "vacation" would rankle. A little good-natured ribbing, perhaps, but Mark wasn't in the mood for it tonight. He gazed toward the far corner of the shop, where another detective was speaking to Robyn. Even from here, Mark could tell that she was making a considerable effort not to look in the direction of Emily's body. Robyn's face was chalky white, and she'd pressed a hand to her stomach, but she seemed determined to do what had to be done. She'd already called her family to break the news of Emily's death, she'd cooperated with the police, and now she was answering more questions. Through it all she'd moved with a dazed, haunted expression on her face, as if hoping this was a nightmare, and any minute now she'd wake up.

Two instincts warred in Mark. He wanted to stay with Tom and learn whatever else he could about Emily Parkman's death. At the same time, he wanted nothing more than to shield Robyn from learning more.

The second impulse won out. Without bothering

to chitchat further, Mark strode across the shop. "Leslie," he said to the detective who'd been speaking with Robyn. "You have enough for now, don't you?"

"Sure, Mark." Leslie gave him a sympathetic look.

Mark shepherded Robyn from the store. She didn't protest, and certainly she didn't look at Emily's body. Out in the parking lot they ducked under the yellow crime-scene tape and went past the police cars. Emily's death had set everything in motion—everyone was doing their job. It occurred to Mark that crime scenes were much like anthills, a whole colony of workers scurrying about: the patrol officers, the detectives, the technicians, the medical investigator, and of course, the inevitable journalists. Mark steered Robyn around a corner just as a TV-station van pulled into the lot.

He walked her down the street, his arm steadying her in the darkness. He could tell she was shaking, and she bent forward a little.

"If you need to be sick," he said, "it's okay."

"No," she whispered, and then her voice came stronger. "Who would do it, Mark? Who would do such a terrible thing? Poor Emily...oh, Lord, maybe I *will* be sick."

They stopped, Mark's arm still around Robyn as she pressed her hand to her stomach yet again.

"It's okay," he repeated. "I remember the first homicide I ever saw. It took me a long time to recover."

"The first..." Suddenly she sounded angry. "There have been plenty of times since, haven't there? This really *is* just a job to you, Mark! People dying, that's what keeps your paycheck coming down at the police department."

He knew that right now she had to be angry at someone, or something, and he was the closest thing available. He waited, still holding her, for her rage to dissipate. Finally, she swiveled toward him and buried her face against his chest.

"I'm sorry," she mumbled. "I know you have to do your job. But I can't stop thinking about Emily. I'll admit I didn't like her. She was always so full of herself—but..." Robyn pressed her face deeper against Mark.

"For what it's worth, I'm damn sorry, too," he said.

"Someone shot her," Robyn said. "It's almost a joke. My father wanted so badly for me to get a gun so I could protect myself, so I could protect Mom—and Emily is the one who ends up...dead. Only it's not a joke. It really happened. I would do anything to make it not happen, Mark! To go back and stop it. Stop whoever it was from lifting a gun and pulling the trigger..."

It took him a minute or two before he realized that Robyn was crying. The tears came silently, and he was only aware of them when they dampened his shirt. He wanted to go back, too, erase the fact of Emily Parkman's murder. He wanted to go back to the time, only a few hours ago, when Robyn had lain on his bed and he'd made love to her. Regret came over him. There would be no going back, not after everything that had happened tonight.

Already Robyn was withdrawing from his arms, making an effort to stand on her own. "How could I forget?" she asked. "Josh...poor Josh. I have to find him, Mark. I have to talk to him before your police friends get to him. I have to be the one to tell him about his sister."

CHAPTER TEN

IN THE END, it was easier than Mark had expected to find nine-year-old Joshua Parkman. Robyn's mother had been able to provide an address on Arvada Street. It was an upscale neighborhood, with houses sequestered behind adobe walls, fashionably weathered gates protecting the entrances. Mark had expected something a little more subdued for the Parkmans, and apparently so had Robyn.

"This can't be right," she said. "Are you sure we wrote down the address correctly?"

"This is it." Mark parked in front of a gate and climbed out to ring the bell—a real bell, a tarnished brass one hanging by a corded rope. It was the kind of rustic charm indulged in only if one had the money to afford the more modern conveniences. Yet, according to Robyn's mother, it had been a struggle for Emily Parkman to support both herself and her brother. This was not an address suggesting financial hardships of any kind.

Robyn came to stand beside Mark. "I'm not looking forward to this. Why can't I stop shaking?"

He pulled the bell cord again. Then he took off his coat and placed it around her shoulders. "The boy has to know sooner or later," he said. "It's best to do it now."

"I wish you weren't such a damn *expert* at all this." Her anger had returned.

"I'm sorry she was killed, Robyn."

She huddled inside his coat. The light from the street lamp picked out the reddish strands of her hair, but it also blanched her skin. "Maybe Josh isn't here," she murmured. "Maybe we really do have the wrong address."

Mark pulled the rope, and sent a clanging sound onto the night air once more. This time it sounded mournful. He put his arm around Robyn again. She didn't lean into him, as she had before, but she didn't move away, either.

At last a voice came from the other side of the gate. "Who's there?" It was a kid's voice, trying hard not to sound scared.

"Josh, are you alone in there? It's me. Robyn Myers. I need to talk to you."

"What are *you* doing here?" Now the voice sounded combative.

"Josh, let me in. It's about...it's about Emily."

No sound at all for a long moment. And then, slowly, the gate creaked open to reveal young Joshua Parkman in a pair of too-big pajamas. His hair was mussed, as if he'd just risen from sleep. He looked from Robyn to Mark and back again, and his expression grew more and more frightened.

"Where's Emily?" he asked in a small voice.

"Josh," Robyn said, "we'd better go inside."

The boy stared at her, but after another few moments he led the way over a brick pathway into the house. Once inside the living room, Robyn encouraged him to sit down on the sofa. Then she knelt in front of him.

"Josh," she said, her voice surprisingly steady, "there's no easy way to say this. Emily...your sister...I'm so very, very sorry, but she's—" The steadiness had lasted only briefly, after all. Robyn didn't seem able to go on.

Mark knelt in front of the boy, too. "Your sister has died, son," he said, knowing there was absolutely no way to soften the words.

Josh's first reaction was predictable. "No," he said. "Where's Emily? I want Emily."

"Josh, I'm sorry, but it's true," Robyn said. "Your sister was killed tonight."

Josh looked at her with a blank expression, apparently still refusing to believe. "Emily's not my sister," he said very calmly. "She's my mother, and I want to see her."

Robyn gave Mark a stunned glance, then turned back to Josh. "It can't be—"

The boy's lip began to tremble. "I want to see my mom. I want to see Emily!"

"Oh, Josh," Robyn whispered. "I'm so sorry..."

Josh's face seemed to crumple. He looked very young, and very frightened. Robyn sat down on the sofa beside him and gathered him into her arms.

"I'm sorry," she murmured over and over. "I'm so terribly sorry."

The boy sobbed. Robyn patted his back, and for a second or two he seemed about to collapse against her. But then, just as quickly, he straightened. He lifted his head, and even with tears trickling down his face he looked belligerent. "I think you should go away," he said. "Emily told me never to let anybody in when she wasn't here."

Robyn stayed where she was, and Mark sat down in a chair next to the sofa.

"Josh," he said. "I need your help, and I know you can be brave. Can you tell me why your mom pretended to be your sister?"

"This isn't the time," Robyn began to protest, but Mark gave her a warning glance.

The boy clenched his hands. "Emily says it's the best way. She says it's so people won't bug us. And she says someday we can move someplace different and then I can call her Mom and everything will be better."

"Josh," Mark said, "did your mom have any special friends I might talk to?"

"I don't know." Josh's face crumpled again, and Robyn gazed accusingly at Mark.

"That's more than enough for now," she said. "Please find something else to do, Mark. I want to talk to Josh on my own." Her voice held unmistakable command, but Mark was reluctant to leave. He knew that some things just couldn't wait, not when a murder investigation was involved. Mark studied the boy. Maybe Robyn was right. Josh wouldn't be able to tell him anything more right now.

Mark rose to his feet and went to one of the adjoining rooms. Now he would have a chance to go through the rest of the house, and see what more he might learn about the Parkmans. That was probably something Robyn wouldn't understand. Her natural reaction, no doubt, was to give death some respect, to back away from it. But Mark had learned all too well that you couldn't back away, not if you wanted to find the truth.

Twenty minutes later he'd made a thorough circuit of the house. All the furnishings appeared to be carefully chosen antiques: rosewood bureaus, a parquetry chest, an unwieldy oak dresser. The portraits on the walls were so dark and murky they could be nothing but originals. Mark found only two rooms that looked as if they'd been lived in recently. One, clearly, was Josh's, identifiable by the heap of clothes on the floor, the comic books stacked with unexpected neatness in a corner.

The other room was the one Emily had obviously inhabited. Here Mark saw an impressive array of clothes in the closet, while the dresser displayed an arrangement of perfumes, makeup, brush and comb. A few paperback novels were stacked on the nightstand. Otherwise there were no personal details.

When Mark made his way back into the living room, he saw that Josh was lying on his side on the brocade sofa, his knees drawn up almost to his chest. A blanket covered him, and his eyes were squeezed tightly shut as he pressed his cheek into a pillow. Right now he looked five years old. When Robyn saw Mark, she motioned him quickly into the adjoining room, closing the door.

"Josh is pretending to be asleep," she said in a low voice. "He can't deal with any more talk." Her tone hardened as she went on. "I can't believe the way you spoke to him. He's just a kid, and he'd barely heard about Emily, but you started asking him questions! What's wrong with you, Mark? Has being a policeman destroyed your emotions?"

"I wish I could make things less rough for the boy," he said. "But there are questions that needed asking. And I was the one to do it."

"He's scared, Mark. Scared and confused. He just heard about Emily being killed—"

"I feel for Josh, too, Robyn." Mark took a step toward her, but she held up her hand.

"No," she said. "Please don't. I just want to think. I want to try to find a way through all this."

She wouldn't take physical comfort from him, and he had nothing else to offer. "I'm trying to think it through myself," he said. "I'm trying to figure out why Emily Parkman pretended that her son was her kid brother."

"I ask myself what kind of mother would foist such a pretense on her own child," Robyn said. "But then I start thinking that she would have been only seventeen or so when he was born. A teenager…"

"I'd like to know how Emily could afford a place like this for herself and Josh," he said. "On the other hand, a little digging into property records could show that the place belongs to someone else. From the look of it, Emily only meant to stop here temporarily."

"From the look of *your* apartment, you only mean to stop there temporarily." Robyn placed both hands at her temples. "Oh, Lord," she said. "What's wrong with me? Listen, Mark, I know you're not the enemy. I really do know that…

She was trying too hard to convince herself, Mark

thought. Right now it seemed that the space between them was immeasurable. He experienced a sensation that it took him a moment to recognize. Loneliness.

"I have to take care of Josh," Robyn said almost to herself. "He doesn't have anyone else."

"Robyn, it's not your place," Mark told her. "Child Services will be involved immediately—"

"No," she said. "That's the last thing he needs right now." She swiveled back toward Mark, and suddenly she looked fierce. "I want to look after Josh. At least he knows me, I'm not a complete stranger to him."

He saw the intensity in her face, and suspected she needed the kid as much as the other way around. Why she felt that way, he didn't know, but he found himself responding to it.

"For what it's worth," he said, "I'll try to stall the authorities, or at least convince them that Josh is better off with you for now. But it's temporary, Robyn. Remember that."

She scarcely seemed to register the last part. "Thank you, Mark," she said formally. "Whatever efforts you can make…thank you."

The bell at the gate rang out, disturbing the stillness of the night air. Robyn gave an explosive sigh. "What now?" she asked.

"Three guesses," Mark said laconically.

"Your friends from the police?"

"That's my guess, anyway." Mark went back through the living room. Josh now sat up on the couch, his shoulders wrapped in the blanket. His eyes were red rimmed, but he managed to glare as Mark went by. A few seconds later, Mark opened the gate to Tom Granger.

"Somehow I'm not surprised to see you here, Stewart."

"Just lending a little help."

"You *are* on vacation, in case you'd forgotten." Tom stepped through the gate, straightened an imaginary wrinkle in his perfectly aligned suit jacket, and went in to take charge of the investigation.

A FEW HOURS LATER, Robyn finally got Josh settled in a spare room at her aunt and uncle's house. Closing the door behind her, she emerged to find her mother hovering nearby.

"You did the right thing bringing him here," Nina said. "When I think of poor Emily…" Tears leaked from her eyes. "Emily was the only family Josh had. I'm still trying to take in that she was his mother…but now he'll have to depend on us."

"Yes," Robyn said. "Yes, he will." If her own nerves felt stretched to the breaking point, the strain had to be even worse for Nina. "You should rest," Robyn told her. "Mark said he'd try to keep his police associates away for a little while, and you need to take advantage of any respite we get. It won't last long, I'm afraid."

"Rest...I wonder if I'll ever rest again," Nina said.

Just then Aunt Janet appeared in the hallway. She held one of her cats tightly against her—a three-legged calico she'd taken in as a stray. Lines of strain were etched into her face.

"Greg's gone," Aunt Janet said in a mechanical tone. "He's left me—just the way he did before. Only this time it's worse...so much worse."

Nina quickly went to put an arm around her. "Oh, Janet...I'm sorry—"

"He's gone," Janet repeated dully. The cat, as if sensing her despair, nestled closer to her.

Nina took charge. "Robyn, dear, will you go check on your father? And meanwhile, I think Janet is the one who needs some rest."

Robyn watched as her mother and aunt went down the hall. Janet was the younger of the two women, but she seemed to have aged in some irrevocable way. It showed in the slump of her shoulders, in the way she bowed her head. How could Uncle Greg have left now? How could he have just walked away...

The events of this dreadful day weighing on her even more than before, Robyn went down the stairs. She searched for her father, and came upon him in the den. Cal was sitting in front of Uncle Greg's desk, staring off into the distance. His arm was still in a cast, his face still bruised. He looked oddly stern.

"Dad, you have to go to bed," Robyn told him. "The doctor said you were to spend most of your time taking it easy."

Cal didn't answer. But the expression on his face became one of such grief that Robyn felt a cold dread seeping through her. She stepped toward him, then stopped.

"Dad," she whispered, "are you okay?"

He didn't answer for quite some time. But then, at last, he spoke. "She shouldn't have died," he said, his voice hollow.

Any number of thoughts raced through Robyn's mind. Her exhaustion had fled, leaving only this dreadful suspicion. "Dad," she said very quietly, "please tell me the truth. You've already admitted to having an affair. Now I need to know...was the affair with Emily?"

She prayed for his denial. She wanted him to say that he was sad only because Emily had been such a young woman, with so much of life still ahead of her. Instead, he merely stared at Robyn, and the grief in his expression told her everything.

"Dad, how could you? *Emily—*"

"You can't tell your mother," he said, his voice breaking. "Please don't tell her."

But Nina had already come down the stairs and walked into the room. "What is it Robyn can't tell me, Cal?" Her own voice was now without emotion. "I think I should hear. I think it's time I knew the truth."

THE REAL ESTATE OFFICE of Randall Garrett and Associates was a place where dreams came true, or so advertised the poster in the window. The poster displayed photographs of several "dream" houses for sale. Mark pushed open the door and went inside.

The place had expensive ivory carpeting, so pristine it made you uneasy—afraid you might be leaving a trail of dirty footprints behind you.

"May I help you?" The woman who spoke gave him a practiced smile. She wore white, too, not a smudge on her. She had blond hair and rather pale skin. Between the room and this woman, Mark could have done with some color right now. It occurred to him that ever since Emily Parkman's murder last night he hadn't been in the best of moods.

"I'd like to speak to Mr. Garrett," he said.

The blonde gave another smile. "I'm afraid Mr. Garrett is out at the moment. I'm his associate, however—Brianne Davie." She held out her hand and he shook it.

She had a limp grip. You'd think that in the real estate business, at least they'd teach you to give a decent handshake. Everything about this woman annoyed him, including her name. Brianne...sounded like some kind of fancy cheese.

"When will Mr. Garrett be back?" Mark asked, his rotten mood making him sound gruffer than he intended.

"I'm not certain. But I'm in charge of everything until he returns. I'm sure I can help you." She studied him carefully. "You rent, don't you?" she asked after a moment.

Mark gave her a dour glance that did nothing to discourage her.

"Let's see," she said, "what do you do for a living, Mr....?"

"I'm with the police."

Even this didn't faze her. In fact, she actually seemed pleased. "Every neighborhood is happy to have a policeman in residence—did you know that? Now, I realize you don't make the most generous salary in the world, not in your line of work, but I have just the place for you." She thumbed expertly through the folders on her desk, extracted one and handed it to Mark. "Go ahead," she urged. "Take a look."

He opened the folder. It contained a sheet detailing a house out in the foothills—acreage, square footage, plumbing and wiring recently overhauled. There was also a photo attached, of a small place half buried among piñon scrub.

"What do you think?" asked Brianne. "It's a bit of a fixer-upper, but that puts it in your price range. Just think of that stunning mountain view."

"Let me get this straight," Mark said. "You're trying to sell me a house."

"Well, of course. Let me tell you, I have very good instincts, Mr...."

"Mark Stewart. Detective Mark Stewart."

"Oh, a detective—even better. Anyway, I have excellent instincts, Mr. Stewart. I know when a client and a house belong together. And you belong with *this* property." She tapped the folder with one of her glossy, colorless nails. Mark found himself studying the photo. The house had green trim and it was surrounded by a low exposed adobe wall.

"Two bedrooms," said Brianne, "with plenty of room to build an addition, if you'd like. That's a generous piece of land. All the potential for a family home, don't you think?"

In spite of himself, Mark found himself trying to put a family in the photo. But all he came up with was a vision of a slender, beautiful woman, her short reddish hair ruffling in the breeze....

He set the folder back on the desk. "I'm interested in a house at 239 Arvada," he said.

"Hmm..." Brianne flipped through the other folders on her desk. "Arvada...two-three-nine. Here it is. This is one of our most select properties." She gave a regretful shake of her head. "Mr. Stewart, it would be quite out of your price range."

"How long has the house been on the market?"

Brianne pursed her lips. "A place like that doesn't necessarily go quickly," she hedged. "One waits until just the right buyer comes along."

"Odd that you don't have a For Sale sign in front of the house," Mark said.

"Our more prestigious clients don't usually need to advertise that way. They would consider it..."

"Vulgar?" Mark supplied, deadpan.

"Yes, that's right. Vulgar."

"Maybe the reason has more to do with practicality," Mark said. "I understand the owners of 239 Arvada are in Europe right now. They wouldn't want to announce their absence with a sign out front. That would be an invitation to burglars and the like."

"Yes, well, that would make sense, wouldn't it?" she asked briskly. "Mr. Stewart, if you don't like the two-bedroom adobe, I can show you several other properties, but believe me, this is the place for you."

"Last night a woman was murdered. Turns out she was bunking at 239 Arvada."

At last it seemed he'd gotten through to Brianne. Her head came up, making her blond curls bounce. "Someone was *murdered*—in the house—"

"No," Mark said. "She was killed at her place of work, but she'd been living at the house on Arvada."

"That's impossible. Our clients trust us to take good care of their properties. We would *never* allow someone to live in one of the houses we're selling."

"Maybe Mr. Garrett knows something about it," Mark said. "You might want to tell him I've been around, and I'll check back to talk with him."

Brianne seemed about to get indignant, but then an almost pensive expression came over her. "The woman who died...who was she?"

"Someone unlucky," Mark said. "Someone very unlucky."

He went out the door, and almost collided with Detective Tom Granger. Tom was wearing another one of his suits. He gave the impression of someone who could actually afford a dream home.

"Stewart. Why am I still not surprised?"

"Brianne is the lady you'll be talking to in there. And watch out...she'll probably end up selling you a house."

Mark climbed into his Land Cruiser. He drove

homeward, intending to call Robyn as soon as he arrived. But when he pulled up at his apartment, he found that wouldn't be necessary. Robyn was sitting right on his front stoop, and close beside her huddled nine-year-old Josh Parkman.

CHAPTER ELEVEN

As MARK WENT UP the walk toward his apartment, Robyn stood and watched him approach.

"Hello, Mark," she said.

"Robyn," he answered.

Josh didn't say anything. The kid's eyes were red this morning, and Mark suspected he'd shed more than a few tears during the night. But his carefully set expression said he didn't want anyone to acknowledge the fact.

Mark's gaze strayed to Robyn. Her russet hair was tousled, her face free of makeup as if she'd had to dispense with the usual amenities. She looked beautiful.

"Mark, we have to talk." She turned to the boy. "Josh, would you mind waiting in the car for a few minutes? You can play the radio as loud as you like."

After a second or two of hesitation, Josh went to the sedan that no doubt belonged to Robyn's parents. He climbed inside, but he didn't seem too interested in the radio. He just sat there with all the windows rolled up, staring out the windshield.

"You've taken on a load of responsibility with him," Mark said.

Her features tensed. "He's just lost his mother. Someone has to look out for him."

"I wasn't accusing you, Robyn."

She gave a sigh. "We just need to talk, Mark. We have other problems. My uncle left the house some-time last night, walked out on my aunt Janet. It's not the first time, and maybe that's why she feels all the more betrayed. But that's not all. The affair my father had—turns out it was with Emily Park-man. I found out about it, and so did my mother." She paused to look at Mark. "Doesn't *anything* ever surprise you, Mark? You're listening as if all of this is just to be expected."

He rubbed a kink in his neck. "I'll admit I didn't connect your father with Emily."

"Apparently it started not long after she began working at the gift shop. My poor mother is dev-astated. She was the one who hired Emily, who took such an interest in her and Josh...and now to find out this. My father keeps telling my mother how sorry he is. Over and over he says it. He swears that he ended things with Emily several weeks ago. As if that's supposed to make it better. You know the funny thing about all this? I start to hate Emily for everything she did, and then I just can't anymore. In spite of everything, I know how she felt about Josh. She loved him, Mark. No matter what kind of crazy life she was giving him, she really loved him. And he loved her, too." Robyn's voice caught.

Until now, Mark had resisted the urge to touch her. He couldn't prevent it anymore, though. He took her hand in both of his.

"I've found out something, too," he said. "I did a little digging, and learned that the house on Arvada Street is for sale. The owners are away, and they've left everything in charge of a real estate firm. I spoke to one of the agents, and asked her why someone was living in the house. She didn't seem to know anything about it, but there's another guy I have to track down. A Randall Garrett— maybe he's the one who gave Emily a key and allowed her to settle in."

"None of it makes any sense," Robyn said. "I mean, who *was* Emily...really?"

"Josh might know the answer better than anyone else."

Robyn stiffened and pulled her hand away. "I'm sure Josh has some things to tell us, but I won't have you interrogating him, Mark. Not right now, anyway. He needs time—he hasn't even accepted yet that Emily is dead."

"Robyn...I understand how you feel. By the way,

I was able to pull a few strings, and you can look after Josh for now. I can't promise for how long, though—''

"It's enough," she said. "Thank you, Mark." After that, she didn't speak for a moment. "We have another problem to resolve," she said. "I'd intended for Josh to stay with my family, but that's out of the question now. My father has just admitted to having an affair with Josh's mother. I know Mom would never blame Josh for any of that, but right now she simply has too much to cope with. She doesn't need anything more. And Josh has enough to cope with, too. Having all of us stay in the same house is asking too much of everyone.''

"I think you're right about that," Mark said.

"Everything in my family is falling apart," she said unhappily. "No one even knows where my uncle is right now. He didn't say where he was going...he just left. And Aunt Janet's not talking much, either. She still won't say what the trouble is between her and Uncle Greg. I'm beginning to wonder if I really know anything about my family.''

Mark knew she wouldn't like what he had to say next. But he had no choice. "Robyn, we have to consider the fact that your uncle left the very night of Emily's murder. I've never been one to believe in coincidence.''

"What are you implying—that my *uncle* had

something to do with it? Uncle Greg, whose only idea of violence is recounting the Battle of Waterloo? He's a military-history buff, not a criminal.''

"You said yourself that maybe you didn't know everything about your family.''

She gave him a stony look. "I know my uncle Greg. He's kind and good-hearted. So just forget your damn implications.''

Mark didn't pursue the subject. Josh wasn't the only one who needed time to come to terms with what had happened. Robyn had every right to be angry. But, when she continued, she spoke with an almost unnatural calm.

"It's my parents I'm trying to understand. I love both of them, no matter what's happened, but...I just don't understand them right now. Neither one of them will own up to the truth. Dad still refuses to say a word about who attacked him, or why he took all that money out of the bank. And when the police came to question my parents, Mom refused to say a word about Dad having the affair. She covered for him as usual. I wish she had more pride.''

"I get the feeling you didn't tell Detective Granger about the affair, either,'' Mark said. "Isn't that covering up?''

"I don't know...maybe,'' she said irritably. "But I'm telling *you* about it, and you're the police, too.''

"Fair enough.'' He studied Robyn, and saw the

emotions struggling across her face. Sorrow, disappointment, disillusionment…her father had let her down, big time. Yet, even now, she still loved her dad. She'd said as much, and Mark could also see it in her eyes. Mark couldn't help thinking about his own two daughters, wondering if they could ever feel that way about *him*…love him no matter what his past mistakes.

Robyn took a deep breath, as if preparing herself for what else she had to say. "Aunt Janet has begged my parents to stay on with her. Especially now, with Uncle Greg gone, she says she needs the company. Mom and Dad, in spite of *their* problems, have agreed. But that still leaves Josh. I've thought and thought about it, and I've realized I have to be the one who looks out for him. I keep seeing the look on his face, when we told him that Emily was dead…and I want to watch out for him. So that means Josh and I stick together. And *that* means we need someplace to stay, someplace safe…I thought about a hotel, but that doesn't feel secure enough. There's another option, of course. Josh and I could stay at my parents' house."

Mark shook his head. "The two of you, inside that big place…I don't like it. With that inner courtyard, the security's not very good. If someone wanted to, they could climb over the roof and get inside."

Robyn held her arms against her body. "You think that's a possibility?"

"Anything's a possibility at this point. We can't discount your father's warning about you being in danger. Your parents could be in danger, too, if the attacker decides to return. But I don't think anyone could get past all the media that's going to be camped on the doorstep. The murder of a beautiful young woman who worked for a well-to-do Santa Fe family...journalists are going to be falling over themselves around your aunt and uncle's house."

Robyn buried her face in her hands. "I don't believe it," she murmured. "Which is worse, my family being hounded by unknown assailants, or by the media... I really want to protect Josh from all this." After a moment she lifted her head. "Mark, I hate suggesting this, I really do. But Josh and I could stay at my parents' house if, well, if you stayed there, too. We'd be safe for sure then."

Mark rubbed that crick in his neck. "Thanks for the vote of confidence...I guess. But you know the press is bound to find out you have the murdered woman's son with you. No doubt they'd love to get some photos of him plastered in the newspapers—and on the six o'clock news. Are you ready for that?"

"God, no. I couldn't possibly subject Josh to that." Robyn was starting to look a little desperate.

"What on earth am I going to do? When it comes right down to it, what I really need is a safe house—I'm sure you'd call it that, anyway."

"A safe house?" he repeated.

"Okay, so maybe I've seen a few too many movies. But that's what the police always call it. And you being a detective and all, you should know about these things."

An idea began to form in Mark's mind. He considered it for a moment, then reached a decision.

"Look, there's another solution. You can stay with me."

Impatiently she pushed a stray wisp of hair away from her cheek. "Mark, I told you—it's not going to happen again. We've already made our big mistake."

"I'm not asking you to go to bed with me," he said. "I'm offering you a place to stay where the press won't hound you, and I'm relatively certain you won't be murdered in the dead of night."

Robyn looked at him as if she thought he had lost his mind. But then she looked over at Josh, waiting in the car.

ONLY A FEW HOURS LATER, Robyn had moved into Mark's apartment.

She couldn't believe it had happened. But Mark had pointed out the logic of the plan: there was really no place else for her and Josh to go. They couldn't stay with her family—not when her father had admitted to an affair with Josh's mother. They couldn't stay at her parents' house—not with reporters waiting to pounce. And Mark was not about to let them stay anywhere alone—not when there was the possibility of them being in danger. His apartment, Mark insisted, although cramped, was the only choice. And, because Mark was not officially connected to the case, the media wouldn't connect Robyn and Josh to him. Robyn couldn't argue with his reasoning.

At this moment, though, she felt overwhelmed by the twenty-four hours she had just gone through. All she really wanted was to bury her head in her hands and generally go to pieces.

She couldn't afford the luxury, though. Right after Mark had installed her and Josh in the apartment, he'd received a phone call from the police department. He hadn't told her what it was about, but his face had turned grim and he'd left. He'd told her to lock the door while he was gone, and had instructed her not to let anyone in. The lock was a solid one, and she really did feel safe here.

She and Josh sat at Mark's dining-room table. It was a card table, if she wanted to be precise about it. But she wasn't about to complain. Now she put a sheet of paper in front of Josh, along with his math book.

"Just try," she said. "The first problem, that's all."

"I'm no good at math," he said.

"Something tells me that you probably are."

"I don't have to do this," he said. "You're not my tutor anymore."

"I'm your friend, Josh."

His lip trembled, and his eyes filled with tears.

"I don't want any friends. I want Emily."

"I know," Robyn said gently. Again she felt a sense of unreality wash over her. She'd never experienced quite this sense of responsibility toward another person. Her parents had always had each other, and her husbands—well, they hadn't needed her. But Josh was totally dependent on her. She knew there were alternatives. Foster care…but she hated the thought of that. She couldn't picture Josh in a foster home, where people might not have the time or the interest to coax him out of that withdrawn manner of his. So far she hadn't been able to coax him herself.

"Try just one problem," she said now. "Just one."

"Why?"

"Because…because it's what Emily would have

wanted. Just like she would have wanted me to go on tutoring you.''

Josh blinked hard against his tears. He picked up a pencil, and for a moment Robyn thought he'd actually try to work the problem. But then he squeezed his eyes shut, and the tears spilled over. He swiped at his face with his sleeve.

Robyn glanced away. ''It's okay to show you care about her,'' she murmured.

''What do *you* know?'' His voice wavered.

''Only that something terrible happened to somebody you loved. Josh…do you know anything about anyone wanting to hurt your mother?'' She'd spoken these thoughts without meaning to. After all, she'd berated Mark for interrogating Josh.

Something about her words seemed to dry Josh's tears. Now he just looked frightened, and Robyn felt a chill deep inside—a sensation that was becoming all too familiar.

''Josh,'' she said. ''What is it? What *do* you know?''

''Nothing.''

''Why are you scared?''

''I'm not!''

''Yes, you are,'' she insisted. ''Do you know someone who wanted to hurt your mom?''

''Nobody. She had lots of friends.''

"Who are these friends?" she asked. "You mean, like girlfriends?"

"No, not girls, no," he said. "I don't know any of them. I don't know who they are."

"But you just told me—"

"They were scary sometimes. I didn't want to know them." Josh stood up so quickly he almost sent the card table toppling over.

"Josh, honey…"

He rubbed his eyes. "I'm tired," he said. "Ever since last night…I've been tired."

Robyn believed she understood. "Come with me," she said. "Mark's put out his sleeping bag for you."

She offered him her hand, and without any argument he took it. They walked together to the second bedroom at the end of the hall. Robyn settled Josh inside the sleeping bag and watched as his eyelids drifted downward. In an amazingly short time, he was sound asleep, his face still streaked with tears. Robyn wanted to smooth away the tears, but it was best to let him rest. He looked so innocent and unguarded. Robyn watched him a moment longer. Then, as noiselessly as possible, she swung the door shut and went back to the living room.

Here she confronted the futon with no mattress and no cushions. Sleeping arrangements for all of them would be haphazard at best. Mark had offered her his bedroom, and he would rough it in the living room. Certainly she and Mark wouldn't share a bed again—she'd made that perfectly clear. And Mark hadn't argued. Just because they would be living together for a few days, that was no reason for the two of them to start getting cozy.

She moaned, and sank into the armchair. Being in such proximity to Mark, after what they'd done last night...making love so impetuously...

"I don't believe it," Robyn said out loud, but the words did nothing to reassure her. She had lain in Mark's arms last night, beseeching him to blot out all the pain. In the end, she had only stirred more bewildering emotions. She had been able to blot out nothing, after all. The problems had remained, harsher ones had followed. Now Emily was dead, and a little boy was motherless.

A knock came at the front door, jarring Robyn. Mark had said not to let anyone in. Maybe if she simply sat where she was, whoever it was would go away. But after a moment or two the knock came again, and Robyn couldn't take the suspense. She tiptoed to the door and peered through the peephole. She saw a young woman standing outside, someone who looked perfectly harmless. After a second or two, Robyn unlocked the door and swung it open.

The young woman studied her. "I'm looking for Mark Stewart," she said.

"He's not here right now, but he should be back soon."

The young woman appeared to think this over. "I see. Well, I'm his daughter."

Robyn felt new interest. "Are you Kerry?"

"Debra."

"Hello, Debra. Look…why don't you come in and wait for him?"

Debra hesitated, but then she stepped over the threshold. "Why not, I suppose. And you are…?"

"I'm Robyn. There's an armchair over there—best seat in the house." Her halfhearted attempt at humor got no response, but Debra sat down in the armchair. Robyn took one of the folding chairs by the card table.

"Your father talks about you a lot," she said.

"Does he really? How interesting." Debra seemed extremely self-possessed. She settled back in the armchair and crossed her legs. Robyn looked for resemblances, and found them. Debra had the same dark hair as Mark, the same well-defined features. Her eyes, however, were brown rather than gray. She wore linen trousers that were fashionably creased, and a tailored blouse. No-nonsense but stylish was the aura she projected.

"Would you like something to drink?" Robyn asked. "There should be a few beers left…I just haven't had the time to make it to the grocery store yet. If beer won't do, I'm afraid we're talking ordinary tap water."

"I suppose water would be fine," Debra said without enthusiasm.

Robyn poured two glasses from the tap, and found some ice cubes in the freezer. She handed one glass to Debra, and sipped from the other as she sat down again. She was still searching for a topic of conversation as Mark's daughter gave her the once-over.

"I didn't know my father was…living with anyone."

Robyn choked on her water.

"Are you all right?" Debra asked, looking surprised.

"I'm—I'm fine." Robyn set down her glass on the card table. "I'm not living with Mark," she said, perhaps too firmly. "I'm just staying here a few days."

"I see." Debra sounded noncommittal, even disinterested, but Robyn felt the need to clarify.

"Your father and I are just…friends."

"I see," Debra repeated.

Robyn wondered what would happen if she told the truth: I did sleep with your father last night…

"I needed a place for a little while," she said instead, "and he offered his help."

"How nice," Debra said.

"He's been a big help, all along."

"That's my father for you," Debra remarked. "Always a big help."

Robyn didn't miss the sarcasm in the young woman's voice. This encounter wasn't going very well. She and Debra sat across from each other in uncomfortable silence. At least, it was uncomfortable for Robyn. Debra proceeded to open the briefcase she'd brought with her, and take out a pad of paper. She scanned some notes on the top page. With some relief, Robyn heard a key turning in the lock. Mark stepped into the room. He looked at Robyn then at his daughter.

"Debra...hello," he said.

"Don't act so overjoyed, Father."

"I am glad to see you—"

"Right," she said. "Don't look so perturbed. Robyn here has already informed me that the two of you are just friends. Not that I'd have any reason to object." Her tone implied that she'd long ago lost any interest in his personal life. "And now—no offense, Robyn—I'd like to talk to my father alone, if you don't mind."

Of course Robyn didn't mind. It didn't take an empath to feel the tension between father and daughter. The two of them really did need to talk.

CHAPTER TWELVE

MARK AND DEBRA ended up taking a stroll together down the block.

"I got the feeling neither you nor Kerry wanted to see me for a long while," Mark said. "It was a surprise to see you here today. Not that I'm not grateful—"

"Father, don't overdo it."

It seemed to Mark she was the one overdoing it, with the "Father" bit. Couldn't one of his daughters, just once, let an inadvertent "Dad" slip out? They walked on for a short time. Mark's neighborhood was composed of apartments, but they were mostly duplexes like his own, making the effort to look like a house without actually being one. There were willows and cottonwoods, neat flower beds and trim squares of grass. It was the kind of neighborhood where you lived if you were either too young or too old to buy a house. Mark didn't feel he belonged in either category. He didn't know where he belonged, that was the problem.

"Speaking of Kerry," Debra said. "I thought we agreed you should keep a low profile."

"You and your mother were the ones who agreed about that," Mark pointed out.

"Your going to see her at school didn't help. It only upset her more."

Upsetting his daughters seemed to be his new specialty.

After a tense pause, Debra spoke again. "This woman in your apartment…she's more than just someone you're helping out, isn't she?" Debra asked. "I mean, you like her, don't you?"

The question threw him a little, and he answered carefully. "Yes, I like her. But I'm not so sure she feels the same about me." No sense in lying to his own daughter. "Any advice?"

Debra only shrugged. "I'm no expert in these matters."

"How's Trevor?" Mark asked.

"In case you're truly interested, I told him our relationship either had to advance or—or it was over. He's thinking about it." She sounded upset, the way she invariably did when talking about this guy.

"Honey, if he's not good enough for you—"

"Anything you say can't help. So, please, don't say it." She made an obvious effort to regain her composure, and then she went on. "I didn't come to see you so we could talk about your romantic foibles, or mine. I'm here on the job.''

"I see." He didn't see at all.

"The paper sent me up here to cover the story on Emily Parkman.''

"You're not a news reporter," he said. "I have a fairly good memory, and I recall you telling me that you handled local sports.''

"I do. But I'm trying to move up. If I do a good job on this story, my editor is sure to see I can handle weightier pieces." She drew her eyebrows together. "Okay, I'm not really up here officially," she admitted. "A friend of mine on the news staff gave me an early lead on this story, all right? There's something about it that intrigues me. I called around, talked to a few of your friends at the police department, and found out you're involved in the case…not so officially, yourself. So I came up from Albuquerque as soon as I could.'' Debra had a look he'd seen often enough, the one she wore when she didn't expect him to understand. It was a mixture of defensiveness and vulnerability, anger and resentment.

"Look, Debra," he said. "I admire your initiative. I've always been proud of the way you go after things, and I want you to succeed in your career. But we're talking about the murder of a girl only a few years older than you. I hate to see you get involved with that in any way."

"Father...I'm not a kid anymore. I'm perfectly capable of handling this. And don't give me that line about protecting me from the seedier aspects of life. I know, I know...you wanted to keep your job separate from your family, and that's why you were never there for us. I've heard it all before. But this is a good opportunity for me. I need your help."

"What are you expecting from me?" he asked. "You want to use me as a source, that it?"

"I don't see why it should bother you," she said. "This is a good chance for me. I've been trying to get a lead on the right kind of story, something that will get me noticed."

He didn't care for the irony. He'd been doing his best to protect Robyn and Josh from the media, and now it turned out his own daughter was the media, pursuing the murder. And there was Debra's career to consider. He felt torn between helping his daughter, keeping her away from the sordidness and protecting Robyn and Josh. He stopped walking, and waited until Debra faced him.

"Debbie, maybe I've said it too many times before, but it's the truth. If there's one thing I don't regret, it's that I've always kept you from the ugliness of my job. I don't intend to change that now."

"Are you saying you won't help me?" she asked.

"I'm your father. And no father wants his daughter anywhere near a murder case."

She gave him a contemptuous glance. "Save the parental concern. What's the real reason? It's just too much trouble to help me, is that it?"

"Debbie, you know better than that." He stopped, seeing the hard, unyielding expression on his daughter's face. He wondered if anything he said would convince her. She wanted to believe only the worst about him.

Now she observed him speculatively. "This seems to be something personal to you. Is that woman in your apartment involved in the case? None of the information I've gathered so far mentions anyone named Robyn, but still...I'm just getting started."

"Debbie," he said again, "I don't want you involved in this case."

She shook her head. "You know, I thought you'd actually be pleased about this. I thought I'd finally found a way for the two of us to relate on some level. Instead, you're waving me aside as always."

"It's not like that," he said. "I want to protect you."

"Oh, sure, Father, you always want to protect somebody. It looks as though your Robyn is the latest protectee. At least you have good taste—she's very pretty."

"Debbie, there are lots of stories besides this murder case, other stories that will advance your career."

"So you won't help me," she repeated.

"No...not on this."

She gave him another disparaging look. "Maybe I shouldn't be so surprised. Maybe I should have expected as much. Foolish me, thinking my father was going to help me. Well, maybe you won't help me, but I *will* get this story. You can count on that...Father." She turned and strode away from him, swinging her briefcase as she went.

WHEN MARK GOT BACK to his apartment, Debra had already driven off, and Josh Parkman was still sleeping.

"I think he'll be out for a while," Robyn said. "It's the only defense he has." She sat down in the armchair, then stood up again. She didn't seem very much at home. "How did things go with Debra?" she asked.

"Not so well," he said. "She's decided she wants to handle the crime beat for her newspaper. According to her, the Emily Parkman case would be the perfect place to start. I tend to disagree...she tends to think I'm stifling her. Seems like nothing I do makes me popular with my kids."

Robyn gave him a sympathetic look, but she

couldn't seem to remain still. She walked restlessly around the living room. Her circuit of the small area brought her next to him. But she quickened her pace and went past, as if determined not to linger in his vicinity. She ended up next to the empty futon frame.

"We need to talk about Josh," she said. "He told me that Emily had a lot of men friends. But he also said these men could be scary. I get the impression that Emily was up to a lot more than having an affair with my father."

"Maybe Josh can tell us more."

"We have go to easy with him," Robyn said. "His well-being has to come before anything else."

"Solving Emily's murder—I'd say that has a lot to do with Josh's well-being."

"The case always comes first for you, doesn't it, Mark?" she said tightly.

It seemed that today he wasn't popular with anyone. "This isn't officially my case. That's why my boss hauled me in today. He wanted to remind me that I was on leave and that I wasn't supposed to interfere with Tom Granger's investigation." Something of an understatement. The captain had used language a bit more forceful. Then, at the end, he'd instructed Mark "to get a life" outside the police force.

"They're shutting you out, is that it?" Robyn asked.

Mark grimaced. "That's the general idea. My boss thinks I still haven't had enough of a break from my so-called 'latest incident.'"

"Let's get this straight," she said, observing him closely. "You're prone to...incidents? What exactly does that mean?"

It wasn't something he liked to talk about, but Robyn's gaze remained intent. He sat down and eased out his sore leg. "This bullet wound," he said. "I got it chasing down a murder suspect on my own. I should have waited for my partner...somehow I didn't get around to it. Let's just say it was considered a breach of the rules."

"Why didn't you let your partner in on it?" she asked.

"In my judgment, he wasn't up to the job." Mark gave another grimace. "He's a rookie, a guy who made detective before he was ready. It was for his own good, he could have got himself killed."

"So instead *you* got a gunshot wound to the leg."

"A minor injury," Mark said.

Robyn nodded slowly. "I'm really starting to understand you. A loner in your personal life, a loner on the job. Apparently, there've been other 'incidents' in the past. You don't want anyone too close, do you?"

He shifted his leg. "I already told you. My partner was too green."

"Why not just admit it? You're happiest on your own."

"That's not true." Even as he spoke the words, Mark knew Robyn was right. "Well," he conceded. "Maybe in the past, but…things could change. I could change. Who knows?"

Robyn shrugged. "People don't change, Mark. Not all that much, anyway. Maybe it's better just to accept yourself the way you are."

"Enough about me," Mark responded, not liking to hear that he was a loner. It sounded so…so *lonely.* One thing, however, couldn't change. The case did have to come first.

"Robyn," he said. "You realize, of course, that I had to tell Tom Granger about your father and Emily."

"I suppose I did expect it, deep down. Certainly I can't excuse my parents—or even myself, for not being up front with him. One of us should have told Detective Granger about the affair. But somehow I thought…I hoped *you'd* realize my father couldn't have had anything to do with Emily's death."

"Maybe Tom Granger and I don't always see eye to eye, but he's a good detective. He'll keep an open mind."

Now her expression went cold. "Dammit, Mark.

In spite of the despicable things my father's done, he would never physically harm another person."

"I'm not the one he has to convince," Mark said.

Robyn stared at him as if he were a stranger. "If nothing else, you have to acknowledge that my father had just gotten out of the hospital. He was hardly in the condition to hurt someone."

"Unfortunately, it doesn't take that much strength to pull a trigger," Mark said in a quiet voice. "But, like I say, Robyn...it's not me your father has to convince. Tom Granger will be questioning him again right away."

"Good for you, Mark. Maybe you're not such a loner, after all. Your loyalty to the police department comes through." Her back held very straight, she turned and walked down the hall. Then she went into his bedroom and shut the door.

This seemed to be the pattern of his life...women walking away from him. Always walking away.

YOUNG JOSH WOKE UP shortly after noon. He said he wasn't hungry, but Mark knew a good meal was in order. He piled Robyn and Josh into the Land Cruiser and took them out for a pancake lunch— sure to be a kid-pleaser. Josh did end up eating most of his blueberry pancakes, even though he didn't have much to say. After they left the restaurant, he sat in the back seat, looking small and miserable and defiant.

Returning to the apartment would be too oppressive right now, Mark decided. He followed his second impulse of the day, and started driving out toward the foothills.

Robyn gave him a reluctant glance. "Mind telling me where we're going?"

"It's a surprise."

She let it go at that, and gazed out the windshield again. He didn't think she would forgive him anytime soon for his part in her family's troubles. Briefly he wondered how it would have been if he'd met her under better circumstances. Would it have been any different for them? Or were there simply too many other barriers? These were useless questions, he knew, and he hadn't invited them. They just kept popping up in his head at inconvenient times.

It didn't take long to reach their destination. Soon Mark pulled up in front of the house Brianne Davie had recommended to him. He climbed out of the Land Cruiser, waiting for Robyn and Josh to do the same.

The house definitely had something special. It was stuccoed a gentle earth brown that blended into the landscape, but the light green trim on the window and door frames added just the right distinction.

The view was something else again: hills of piñon and juniper rising to meet the crystalline blue of the sky, and then, high above, the peaks of the Sangre de Cristos, still capped with snow. Imagine that, a real estate agent who hadn't overstated her case. Mark was glad that he'd taken note of the address in that folder she'd handed him.

"What do you think?" he asked Robyn.

"It's very nice," she said, but her tone was reserved. She glanced at Josh, who had wandered over by a woodpile next to the adobe wall. "Mark and I are going to have a look around," she told the boy. "We won't be going far. Can you stay right here, Josh?"

He nodded as if it didn't matter to him either way. Then he plunked himself down on the grass and leaned against the wall. He looked very much alone, sitting there, and Robyn gave him a worried frown. But apparently, what she had to say to Mark couldn't wait. She went around the side of the yard and waited for him to follow her.

"Okay, Mark," she said. "So what's this all about?"

He didn't answer her for a moment, just stepped up to a window and cupped his hands so he could see inside. Wooden floors...always a plus. High ceilings, another plus. And a rounded kiva fireplace in the corner, complete with brick hearth. During the winter months, that woodpile would get some use.

"Needs repainting, that's all," he said.

Robyn came to peer in the window, too. "Mark...what *is* this about?"

"I guess you got me thinking today. You mentioned needing a safe house. When I was a kid, if you'd asked me what a safe house was, I would've told you I lived in one with my parents and my brother and sister. A place with people I could count on. Yeah...that would've been my definition. Too bad you grow up and forget about things like that."

Robyn gave him a considering look. "What are you getting at?"

"Hell, I'm thinking about buying a house. Maybe even this house."

"I didn't know you were in the market," Robyn said.

"Neither did I," he said. "But Ms. Brianne Davie of Randall Garrett and Associates seems to think this is the place for me. According to her, she has instincts about this type of thing." He perused the house some more. It had a side porch with torn screens. If you wanted to, you could do away with the screens entirely, just let the open air come in. Or better yet, put in some glass walls, make it into a regular sunroom.

He turned back to Robyn. "What do you think of it?" he asked again.

"What I think of it isn't important right now. What we have to think about is a little boy who's just been through a terrible trauma—"

"I have been thinking about it," Mark said. "Everything that's happened has given me a hell of a lot to think about. Emily's death, the son she left behind... Robyn, you've accused me of losing my emotions because I'm a policeman. In the past, maybe that's been true. Maybe I've seen too much violence, been hardened to it. But last night, I saw a little boy's world crumble around him. I saw how it affected you, and that got to me, too. Life is short. And maybe it shouldn't be wasted."

She gazed at the house, then at him. Her expression was wary. "I don't know where you're going with this, Mark."

"Sometimes I look around," he said, trying to explain, "and all I see is the shrapnel of my life. Fragments...no real home, two daughters who don't want anything to do with me. I guess you could say I'd like a second chance. An opportunity to start over and do things right this time. There's definitely an appeal to that."

"And buying a house, that's a second chance?"

"Maybe it's a beginning," he said. "Maybe it's a statement of faith in the future. Or maybe it's only an unrealistic grab at the past. You start wanting the kind of home you had as a kid, but you don't know how to get it. I'm no authority on any of this."

Robyn's expression grew wistful. "I guess I know what you're talking about. Maybe that's what I've been chasing in my own life. I've wanted a home that would make me as happy and secure as the one I had growing up. Only, I haven't known how to get it. I ended up marrying two men who were wrong for me, and now...now the family that gave me so much security is falling to pieces..."

"So tell me, Robyn. Do I buy the house?"

She drew her eyebrows together. "I certainly can't advise you. I don't know why you'd want my opinion, anyway—"

"We made love last night," he said. "If I've asked a woman to share my bed, then I don't mind asking for her opinion."

The flush came back, full force. "Mark, we've already discussed this—"

"Right, right. It was a mistake. But I still want to know what you think of the house."

She hesitated for a minute or two, obviously unwilling to give in. But then, at last, she turned to examine the place. Mark studied it again, too. It was definitely on the small side, but here and there a detail caught his attention: an unexpected but pleasing scallop design in the outline of a wall, the sturdy wooden columns of the porch, the rough-hewn tiles of the patio. The architectural design was a hodge-podge of styles…a little bit Pueblo, a little bit Territorial, maybe even a touch of Spanish revival. Somehow it all added up to a relaxed, welcoming atmosphere. This was a house that invited you to come in and make yourself comfortable. He wondered if Robyn saw the place the same way he did. But when she turned back to him, her expression was neutral.

"It's nice," she said. "Real nice. But you haven't even checked the inside yet. If I were you, Mark, I'd do a little comparison shopping before I made up my mind."

"You're right, of course," he said. "And I would check the interior if I had the key." He surveyed their surroundings once more, then said, "With this amount of acreage, you could build an addition. Problem is, it's the kind of place for a family. Enough room for a swing set, even an outdoor pool. Kids would love it."

"Thinking of expanding, are you?" Robyn asked lightly.

"Family…I'm no good at families," he muttered. "It's a shame to waste a place like this, that's all I'm saying." He told himself that Brianne Davie would be able to find someone else to buy the house—someone with a couple of children, no doubt.

But it didn't matter what he told himself. He kept picturing himself in this house. And somehow he kept picturing Robyn here, too. She and the house seemed to fit together in ways he couldn't explain. Definitely no logic to it. If he was considering a permanent home at all, she shouldn't be anywhere in the picture.

Mark uttered a curse under his breath.

"Shop around, Mark," she told him gently. "It's always best."

That was the problem. He didn't know what was best for himself anymore. He just knew that he was becoming all too aware of how alone he was, and he didn't like it.

CHAPTER THIRTEEN

LATE THAT NIGHT, Mark decided that sleeping in an armchair was an art he had yet to master. Stretched or scrunched, no matter what he tried, he couldn't get comfortable. And wearing jeans and a T-shirt didn't help, either. Mark was accustomed to sleeping in the raw, but with a full house that wasn't advisable. Finally he gave up even trying to doze, and clicked on the lamp beside him. The empty futon frame across the room seemed to mock him. He'd bought the thing at a furniture sale, intending to outfit it with the appropriate cushions so it could serve as a couch. Somehow he'd never gotten around to it. He'd never needed any extra furniture until now.

He glanced into the shadows down the hall, where two closed doors announced that he was not alone in his apartment. After a desultory supper of canned chili, Josh had gone to bed early. Somewhat later, Robyn and Mark had each retired for the night. There'd been a tension between them that had not vanished just because Robyn had gone into the other room and shut the door. Mark could feel it now, compounded of so many elements he hardly knew how to tell them apart. Lingering desire, discontentment, wishes unfulfilled...

Mark reached down and took his notepad and pen from the floor. Work had always been his best distraction in the past; why should it be any different now? Maybe he wasn't supposed to have anything to do with the Emily Parkman case, but following rules wasn't his forte. He read some of the notes he'd already made on the case: "Randall Garrett?? Robyn's father?? Boyfriends?" Right now nothing was falling into place. Wasn't it still a little too much of a coincidence that Robyn's uncle Greg had walked out on his wife the night of Emily's murder? For that matter, what about the attack on Robyn's father, and the way he'd wiped out that savings account? What was the connection with Emily Parkman? Again, Mark didn't believe in coincidence. Exactly what had gone on in Emily's private life? She'd had an affair with Robyn's father, but who were the other men in her life?

He heard one of the bedroom doors open, and a few seconds later Robyn appeared from the hall. She was wearing a plaid robe belted firmly at the waist, but he still saw a hint of lace at her neckline. Lace nightgown? Lord...he almost jotted that on his notepad.

"Can't sleep?" he asked.

"No." She came farther into the room, and he swore he could hear the rustle of lace. He had to keep his imagination from getting away from him.

"First night in a strange apartment," he said. "Bound to make you a little restless."

She wandered to the window, tilted the blind, peered into the darkness. "I can't believe it was only last night. I feel like I've aged a million years since then."

Maybe she felt bad, but she didn't look bad. Plaid became her. She ran a hand through her hair, and now it was more rumpled than he'd yet seen it. Rumpled became her, too.

"They always say hot milk is supposed to make you sleep," he said. "Maybe you should give some a try."

"I'm surprised you even have milk," she said. The implication remained unspoken: the bare fridge represented his solitary life all too well.

They gazed at each other in the soft lamplight, and Mark found himself looking for more hints of lace.

Robyn glanced away. "I came out here because I figured you probably couldn't sleep, either. I'm a guest in your place. Why don't you take the bed, and I'll take a turn in the chair."

"I'm doing okay."

"You're not sleeping," she said.

"Not much chance of that," he acknowledged.

She sighed, and sat down in one of the folding chairs. "I guess you haven't entertained a lot of overnight guests here."

"The relationships I've had since my divorce...they haven't gone much of anywhere. Actually they haven't even qualified as relationships."

"You and I are the opposite, then," Robyn said. "My relationships always go too far. I end up walking down the aisle, when I ought to be walking out the door."

"So...the ex-husbands," Mark said. "Who were these guys, anyway?"

She cinched the belt of her robe a little tighter. "I'm sure you don't really want to know."

"I asked, didn't I?"

Mark eased back in the armchair, stretching out his leg as best he could. He suspected Robyn had mentioned her trips down the aisle for a reason. He wasn't getting any sleep...wasn't going anywhere.

"Look," Robyn said, "when I met my first husband, it's like I told you—I was at college, away from home for the first time. I was trying to be independent and didn't really know how to go about it. I floundered quite a lot. Anthony had known forever that he wanted to be a lawyer, and his focus drew me. I found out too late he didn't have room for much of anything besides his career."

"And you're telling me this because I remind you of Anthony."

"Not in the least. I know you're totally centered on your own career, but I think you genuinely want to help people—even if your methods are a bit brusque at times. Anthony was a lot more concerned about carving out a position for himself."

Mark thought he'd been complimented…almost. He wouldn't let it go to his head, though.

"No, you and Anthony aren't alike at all," Robyn said. "What's similar in both situations is *me*. Like I told you, I get in a vulnerable position, and I just start depending too much on a man."

In spite of himself, Mark couldn't help being curious. "What about husband number two?" he asked.

"I was vulnerable all over again," she said, sounding as if she was accusing herself. "And I already told you the first part of *this* story. I was on the rebound after a bad attempt to get back together with my first husband…enter Brad. He seemed totally the opposite of Anthony. Had a decent job but wasn't obsessed by it. Relaxed, easygoing. So easygoing, in fact, that after a while he didn't see the need to put any work into our relationship. Exit Brad, some five months ago."

Mark heard the way she tried to be flippant. But he also detected the hurt underneath. "Robyn—"

"You're starting to sound sympathetic, Mark. Don't—it's a bad idea." She stood. "I'd give anything to break the old patterns. Why can't I figure it out?"

"I don't see that my helping you solve a family crisis is the old pattern—being too dependent on a man. I'm a detective, Robyn. It's my job, it's my life. Why can't you just accept my help and stop feeling bad about it?" He stood, too, and came over to her. She seemed about to step away, but then she held her ground.

"It's one thing to accept your help, Mark, but the rest of it..." Her voice trailed off. They gazed at each other again. And then, gently, he cupped her face. It was the most natural gesture...the thing that, underneath all their conversation, he'd been wanting to do.

"Mark," she whispered. It sounded like an entreaty. Did she want him to stop, or go on? She placed her hand on his chest, as if to stay him. But after a moment she ran her fingers over his T-shirt. Another moment later, she gave a sigh, a sound almost of defeat. And then she offered her lips to his...

And just then, a frightened yell came from down the hall.

IT WAS ONLY a matter of seconds before Mark and Robyn made it down the hall and into Josh's room.

Instinctively, Mark kept Robyn behind him as he flipped on the light switch. Josh was sitting straight up in the sleeping bag, breathing in gulps and looking around wildly. He was sweating, his hair damp at the forehead.

Robyn went to kneel beside him, putting her arm around his shoulders. "What is it, Josh?"

The kid stared at her, as if trying to focus on her features. And Mark saw the recognition pass across the boy's face, the moment of remembering that his mother was dead. It showed in the sudden, terrible emptiness in Josh's eyes, the tightening of his hands on the sleeping bag.

Robyn, it seemed, understood the look in Josh's eyes, too. She gathered the little boy close, holding him as if *she* longed to be his mother. "It's okay," she murmured. "It's okay. You had a nightmare, didn't you?"

Josh nodded.

"Might do you good to talk about it," Mark said.

"Somebody was chasing me," Josh mumbled.

Mark and Robyn exchanged glances. "Can you remember anything else?" Robyn asked gently. "Do you know who was chasing you in the dream?"

"No," Josh said, "but I was scared. And I started yelling, and nobody could hear."

"We heard you," Mark said in a reassuring tone. "You've got a good set of lungs on you."

"What did I say?" Josh asked cautiously.

"It was sort of a cross between a screech and a yowl," Mark informed him.

"Really?" For a minute the kid looked impressed. But then he burrowed against Robyn as if to shut out all the bad memories. She held him, and rocked him a little.

"It's okay," she repeated. "Everything's going to be okay." She and Mark exchanged glances again across Josh's tawny mop of hair. It was anybody's guess what the boy had gone through in his nine short years of life. And now, his mother was dead, and he was waking up with nightmares... No little boy should have to go through this. More than ever, Mark wished he could change things for Josh.

"Guess what," Robyn said. "I know the perfect cure for bad dreams. We're all going to have a cup of hot milk." She gave Mark another meaningful glance.

"Yeah, right," he said. "I'll get it started. Hot milk." It was a poor substitute, when he'd been on the verge of kissing Robyn. He felt a stirring of disappointment. He wondered if Robyn would give him another chance to kiss her.

Somehow he doubted it.

THE MORNING after Josh's nightmare, Robyn stepped inside her aunt and uncle's house. The place looked as homey as ever—the sofa covered with a bright, India-print spread, Aunt Janet's collection of music boxes displayed in a cabinet, one or two antiques in the process of refinishing, an elderly mutt named Pete taking a nap on the hall rug, one of the cats perched on the windowsill. With such pleasant surroundings, this should have been a place of contentment...of family togetherness. But Robyn could sense all the troubles beneath the facade.

She found her mother in the kitchen. Nina sat at the table with her hands wrapped tightly around a mug of coffee. Her brooding expression changed when she looked up and saw Robyn. As if slipping on a mask, she gave a determined tilt to her chin. "Hello, dear. It's good to see you. Pour yourself a cup of coffee and sit with me."

Mark was waiting for Robyn outside; she'd only come here to check briefly on her parents. But when she saw the sadness in her mother's expression—the sadness Nina couldn't quite hide—Robyn knew she couldn't leave right away. She poured a cup for herself and sat opposite her mother. "How are you holding up?" she asked. "I know the police have been back to question you."

"Yes...about your father's affair with Emily."

Nina spoke in a distant tone. "It's in the open now, isn't it?"

"Mom, I'm so sorry," Robyn said. "I didn't want to tell Mark about it, but I had to. And of course, he had to tell Detective Granger."

"Yes, dear, of course. You only did what was right." Nina gave a mirthless smile. "It had to come out, didn't it? Your husband sleeps with a woman who ends up murdered, and of course it must come out." Now her voice was brittle, sounding as if any moment it would break into a thousand pieces.

Robyn pulled her chair closer and put her arm around Nina for a moment. "Oh, Mom, I really am sorry—"

"Detective Granger insists there has to be a connection between the murder, and the attack on your father, and the money he took out of our savings...yes, I did tell the detective about the money. I'm not covering up anything anymore. It's your father who still refuses to tell everything."

"This must be really hard on you, Mom," Robyn said inadequately.

Nina made a visible effort to gain control of her emotions. "What about you?" she asked. "Where's poor Josh?"

"Mark has a friend with two boys of his own, and he volunteered to take Josh for the day. They're going to a birthday party at Hannett Park. It seemed like a good distraction, and we'll pick him up there later this afternoon.'' Robyn had worried about letting Josh out of her sight, but Mark had assured her that Benjamin, his friend from the shooting range, was a most competent person who would make sure nothing untoward happened to the boy. Benjamin himself had once been a member of the police force, after all. Besides, Mark had argued, Josh desperately needed to get out and have a little healthful activity. Robyn hadn't been able to disagree there.

''What a very decent man your Mark is,'' Nina said. ''I can't tell you how glad I am that you found him, particularly at a time like this.''

''Mother, he *is* decent, but it's not what you think.'' No, it wasn't what Nina thought, despite the fact that last night Robyn had almost gone into Mark's arms again.

She became aware that her mother had spoken, and was looking at her expectantly, waiting for an answer.

''I'm sorry, Mom,'' she said guiltily. ''I was…thinking about something else.''

''I was just telling you how concerned I am for Janet.''

''No word yet from Uncle Greg?'' Robyn asked.

''Not a thing. And yet…I have a suspicion Janet knows where he is. Maybe she's just too proud to go to him. What could be so bad that they can't work it out?''

"Mom, is that how you feel about Dad?" Robyn asked.

Nina's expression immediately grew shuttered. "That's between me and your father."

It seemed a lifetime habit couldn't be easily broken. Nina was still protecting Cal. And, meanwhile, secrets were still being guarded.

"Mom," Robyn said urgently. "Emily is dead. Before someone else gets hurt, make Dad tell the truth—all of it."

Nina set down her coffee cup with a thump. "Stop, Robyn. Detective Granger has questioned us over and over. I've told him as much as I know. What else can *I* do?"

Robyn's heart ached for her mother. But it was impossible to turn back now. "Mom, I know it's hard," she said, "but there's no such thing as just a little truth. Dad has to tell us everything—or there may be no way to save this family."

"He won't confide in the police. He says even less to me."

Robyn felt a growing futility. She couldn't give up, though—not yet. Leaving her mother in the kitchen, she went upstairs to the room where her father lay propped against pillows. He was awake, but he scarcely acknowledged Robyn's presence. A look of despair seemed permanently etched into his features. The truth was hidden somewhere underneath.

Robyn stepped through the door. "Hello, Dad," she said.

His gaze flickered toward her. "Robyn."

"How are you feeling?"

"I wish I'd been the one to die," he said, his voice low. "Do you know that? I wish I'd been the one." He delivered these words flatly, without varnish, and that made them all the more chilling.

Robyn pulled a chair up beside the bed. "Dad, how can you say that? You won't solve anything by just giving up. Start telling us what happened. It's the only way!"

At first she thought her pleas would have the usual effect: her father would turn his face from her, and he would refuse to say another word. But this time, after a long moment, he began to speak.

"I know what you're wondering the most, Robyn. Why did I do it? Why did I hurt your mother that way? I've been thinking about it. Trying to find excuses, perhaps. Trying to rationalize, for certain. The best I can come up with is that I'm getting old, Robyn. And what's worse, I was starting to feel old. I don't know, perhaps it was the way Emily looked at me, at least in the beginning. As if she could see beneath all the years. As if my life was just beginning again, not nearing the end."

"But, Dad," Robyn couldn't help protesting, "you're not old. And the way I remember it, that's exactly how Mom looked at you. As if you were always in your prime.''

''Your mother has been a wonderful wife. She's not to blame in any of this. The fault's in me, Robyn.''

''Did you...love Emily?'' she asked, her voice soft now, even though it was a question she dreaded asking.

''Do you love someone who makes you feel like you're powerful and strong again?'' he asked. ''I don't know...maybe, for a little while. Maybe I just loved the vision of myself that Emily gave to me. But it was never real. Emily only pretended to admire me. She was setting me up.''

''What do you mean, Dad? How could she do that—''

''Emily blackmailed me,'' Cal said. ''She was smart—she took her time about it. A pretty young woman, turning the head of a man who's scared of getting old... She waited until she had me right where she wanted me, and then she said she'd tell Nina all about the affair unless I paid up.''

The chill inside Robyn spread to every inch of her body. ''Dad, do you realize what you're saying?'' she whispered.

''I know how it sounds,'' he said. ''It sounds like I had a motive to kill Emily.'' Her father went on, his voice oddly expressionless. ''Maybe nothing matters anymore. Emily's gone, and your mother knows about the affair anyway. I don't think she can ever forgive me.''

"She hasn't left. She's standing by you—"

"No, Robyn. In her heart she's already left. What else can I expect? I never wanted her to know…I never wanted to hurt her. But I have hurt her terribly, and that's changed everything.'' He sounded as if he had traveled to some dark place from which he could never emerge. "I don't think I can talk anymore,'' he said. "It doesn't do any good to talk about it.''

Maybe he was right, Robyn thought. For sure she didn't want to know more. She didn't think she could bear it.

She left him, went out into the hall, and almost bumped into Janet. Her aunt seemed to have been listening at the door. She made no move to disguise the fact. She simply stood there, holding another of her cats, this one a striped kitten that she'd saved from the pound.

"What's to become of us all,'' she murmured.

"I don't know, Aunt Janet. I just don't know.'' With that, Robyn went down the stairs and outside to Mark.

CHAPTER FOURTEEN

ROBYN CLIMBED into the Land Cruiser.

"You seem shook up," Mark said. "You want to tell me about it?"

"Oh, well, let's see," she said. "I just found out that Emily was blackmailing my dad, threatening to tell my mother about the affair. And maybe, just maybe, that gave him a strong motive to kill Emily—" She couldn't go on. Mark put his arm around her and pulled her next to him.

"Hey," he said, "we'll get to the bottom of this."

"You sound the way I did last night, trying to comfort Josh after his nightmare. But when will *this* nightmare ever end, Mark?"

He didn't answer. He just went on holding her. She wished he would hold her forever...all the more reason she had to pull away.

He studied her for a minute or two, but then started the engine.

"I made a call while you were in there," he said,

nodding toward his cell phone. "You and I have an appointment."

"Where?" she asked.

"You'll find out soon enough." Mark swung out into the street. He drove quickly, and Robyn had to hold on to her seat as he took a corner. He held the wheel comfortably and easily, but he seemed intent on his own thoughts. Maybe he was considering the new information about Robyn's father. By now Robyn knew how much Mark liked working out the details of a case.

Lost in her own disturbing thoughts, only gradually did Robyn realize that Mark was heading for the foothills.

"We're not going back there, are we...to the house?"

"I didn't think you'd mind so much," he said. "We have a chance to see the inside of the place, and maybe accomplish something else at the same time."

"Mark, don't be mysterious. Goodness knows, I've had enough of that. What are you talking about?"

"Let's just see how it works out," was his only reply. In a short while, they were traveling along the narrow, winding road that led to the house. There were other dwellings scattered about, but the sense of spaciousness did not diminish. And there, tucked among the gentle hills, was the snug, topaz brown house with the green trim. With great reluctance, Robyn had to admit how much she liked the place. Everywhere she glanced, she saw the possibilities. That uneven patch of ground over there could be smoothed out and made into a generous vegetable garden. The woodpile could be restocked for long winter evenings by the fire. The adobe wall all around the perimeter should be left just as it was, although one could plant some lady's slippers and buttercups along the border...

Robyn curled her fingers in her palms, disgusted with herself for thinking this way. *She* wasn't in the market for a house. When Mark brought the Land Cruiser to a halt, she climbed out and followed him as he went along the path toward the front door. She tried not to notice the patterned bricks of the path, tried not to imagine how some wicker lawn furniture would look arranged on the porch.

"I've seen enough," she said.

"What bothers you so much, Robyn?" he asked. "It's just a house."

It wasn't just any house. It was a place that all too clearly asked to be a home.

"I would really like to get out of here," she muttered. But, even as she spoke, a large expensive sedan came down the road and pulled up behind the Land Cruiser. A man emerged from it and came toward Mark and Robyn. In his mid-thirties or so, he had a tall, heavy-shouldered build. He was handsome, if you liked the blue-eyed, sandy-haired type with features almost too perfect. First he shook Robyn's hand, then Mark's.

"Mr. and Mrs. Stewart," he said. "Glad to meet you."

"We're not married," Robyn said, perhaps too hastily.

"My mistake," the man said, not seeming particularly concerned about it. "I'm Randall Garrett, and I'll be happy to show you around. Nice house, isn't it?"

It took Robyn a second to register the man's name. Randall Garrett…the real estate agent who might or might not know something about Emily Parkman. She glanced quickly at Mark, but his expression warned her to let him take the lead. Garrett opened the door to the house and ushered her inside. Mark came in after.

The three of them walked through the place. Garrett pointed out all the details Robyn could see quite plainly for herself.

"Cove ceilings…these oak floors are in very good shape…this is what I like to call a breakfast nook…"

Inside, the house was just as appealing as outside. The master bedroom had an inviting window seat, the closets had double doors that gave a feel of airiness, and the breakfast nook more than made up for the lack of a formal dining room. Mark, while keeping an impassive expression, also seemed to note these features.

"If the two of you would like to stroll around by yourselves," said Garrett, "be my guests. I'll wait outside." The man was being admirably low-key...attempting no hard sell. But Robyn did not want to be alone in this house with Mark. She couldn't afford to allow the place—or Mark—to seduce her.

"No, thank you," she said. "I've seen enough." She went outside, and the two men had no choice but to follow her.

"I have several other properties I can show you," said Garrett. "If this one isn't exactly right, you shouldn't be discouraged."

"Mark and I aren't up for any more today," Robyn said firmly. "*Are* we, Mark?"

He retained that maddening, impassive look. "This is the house we're interested in," he said. "No need to go further. Besides, it's time to talk about Emily Parkman." He mentioned the name in an offhand manner, almost like an afterthought, but it had a distinct effect on Randall Garrett. The man froze for a second or two, losing the urbane good-naturedness he'd exhibited until now.

And then, just as quickly, he seemed to relax again. He gave Mark an inquiring glance. "Just who are you, Mr. Stewart?"

"I'm a police detective."

"I've already spoken with the police…but you must be the one Brianne was telling me about. The guy who showed up at the office yesterday, before the other police. She didn't appreciate being questioned twice. It's just too bad she didn't mention your name to me, or I might have made the connection." A certain look went across his face. *Displeasure* might be the best word to describe it. Robyn only knew that it was a disagreeable look, one that made her glad she wasn't alone with the man.

"I did talk to Brianne," Mark said, "and now I'd like to talk to you. Let's make it simple. Just tell me what you know about Emily Parkman."

"I've given the police all the information they need." Garrett's low-key manner had completely vanished. He didn't appear quite so handsome anymore, not with that unpleasant look on his face. Robyn glanced at Mark. She saw how calm he remained, yet she sensed a readiness in him, too.

"Let's try it this way," Mark said. "I'll do the talking, and you tell me if I'm right. It seems you let Emily stay at the house on Arvada Street. Who knows, maybe that's a habit of yours, letting pretty young women camp out in the homes you're trying to sell. Your clients probably wouldn't be too happy to find out about it, but maybe that's beside the point."

"Emily needed a place to stay, and I helped her out. But I wonder just who the hell you are, and why the hell you think I have to put up with any of this—"

"Did you kill Emily Parkman, Mr. Garrett?" Robyn found herself asking. He turned toward her with a menacing attitude, but at the same time Mark stepped protectively in front of her.

"Take it easy, Garrett," he said. "Just answer the question."

Randall Garrett stood very still for a moment. But then, unexpectedly, his muscles seemed to go lax. Robyn could almost see the fight drain out of him.

"Kill her...why would I do that?" he said, an emptiness in his voice. "How could I have possibly killed her? I loved her with all I had."

LATER THAT MORNING, it seemed impossible to Robyn that all the ordinary details of life could continue. Surely events such as Emily's death and her father's betrayal should make everything else come to a standstill. It didn't happen that way, of course. Ordinary, mundane details did have to go on. Things like shopping, for instance. She and Mark had certain basic purchases to make. After a few hours, they

returned to Mark's apartment not only with three
bags of groceries, but with a full-size futon mattress.
Most of the groceries went in the fridge, and then
Mark and Robyn lugged the mattress into his living
room. Mark pulled out the futon frame until it lay
flat, and the mattress landed on top.

"At least you won't have to try sleeping in an
armchair tonight," Robyn said.

"No, I suppose not." Mark gazed at the futon
regretfully, and Robyn wondered what he was thinking. Maybe his thoughts matched her own. Sleeping
arrangements all made...no possibility now that they
would need to share a bed tonight...

She pushed the inappropriate thought away.
"Well, what's next?" she asked briskly. "There
must be something more we can learn about Randall
Garrett. I think it's possible he's the one who killed
Emily."

"Robyn, I have a feeling that right now you'd
accuse anyone, rather than believe your father did
it."

"Can you blame me?" she asked. "Maybe a lot
of my illusions about my father have been destroyed, but at least let me hang on to this one. Let
me believe in his innocence." If only she was convinced of it herself! But Cal could have been desperate enough to have done it. Despite his injuries,

he could have made his way to the gift shop that night. And he could have pulled a trigger...

Mark came over to her. "You need a break from all this," he said. "For at least a little while, you need to forget about everything that's happened."

She curled her fingers inside her palms. "I can't forget, and I know you can't, either. The case is what matters, isn't it?"

"Yes," he said. But he looked at her as if he felt sorry for her. She didn't want his pity.

"There must be something else we can do," she said. "Something else we can check out. Other leads to follow."

Mark simply went on looking at her, and she saw another expression cross his face. Her heartbeat accelerated.

"Will you please *stop* making love to me with your eyes," she said. "We can't make another mistake. We just can't."

"Was it really such a mistake?"

"You know it was—"

"Perhaps," he said gravely. "Or perhaps we should just admit how we feel." His eyes held hers. Robyn could no longer deny the need for honesty. Recent events had torn from her the possibility of pretense.

"Dammit, Mark, of course I want to...be with you. Of course I want to forget everything else—"

"Is that the only reason?" As always, he could be relentless.

She took a deep breath. She wanted to stop this conversation right now. But honesty was a peculiar thing. Once you started, it wasn't easy to stop.

"I'll tell you what frightens me, Mark. Maybe it's not only escape I want. Maybe I'm starting to feel something else for you. And that's very dangerous. Because this is the wrong time, the wrong circumstances to start feeling anything. How can I possibly sort it out..."

He took a step closer to her. And then he kissed her.

A long moment later, they broke apart. Robyn felt her pulse beating in her throat. "It's not fair," she whispered. "You know what you're doing to me..."

"I know what you're doing to me," he answered.

Robyn was the one who reached out, running her fingers over his shirt. She felt the steady rise and fall of his breath. Then he covered her hand with his, cupping it next to his chest. An ache of longing grew inside her, and she could not deny it. She leaned close to Mark, brought her lips to his again.

They kissed for another long moment, and then another. Robyn told herself to stop before it was too late. But she knew, deep down, that it was already too late. Somehow, in all the pain and uncertainty that surrounded her, she had come to this...she had come to Mark. There would be no turning back. It was as if she had surrendered to the currents of desire, letting them sweep her where they would.

Together they sank onto the futon mattress. And now the caresses began. Mark's hands, tracing the line of her back…her fingers twining in his hair… She gave a sigh as his hand strayed across her hip, found its way beneath her blouse. Mark had worked his magic on her, and every touch bound her deeper under this spell of desire. The early-afternoon sunshine spilled over them, slanting its way in through the blinds, and this alone stirred a faint remnant of modesty inside her.

"Mark…the windows…"

"I'll take care of it," he murmured. He left her to draw the curtains over the blinds. And then he disappeared down the hall, going into his bedroom. She heard a bureau drawer open then close. When he appeared again, he brought a condom packet with him. Everything about his demeanor was matter-of-fact. The sun still managed to find its way around the edges of the windows, giving more than enough light for Mark and Robyn to see each other.

He took off his baseball jacket and tossed it over a chair back. Next came the shoulder holster—that ended up draped on a chair back, too. His shirt, his shoes and socks…

"Mark," Robyn said.

He came to lie beside her again. As he unbuttoned her blouse, and then helped her tug her camisole over her head, his gaze lingered upon her.

"You're beautiful," he said. When she tried to go into his arms again, he stopped her. "No," he murmured. "Let me look at you. Why do you turn your head away? You're not ashamed, are you? Because you really are beautiful."

She felt the color heating her cheeks. "I'm not used to having someone take time…to look."

"Anyone who didn't take the time was a fool. I want to look at you, Robyn. And I want you to enjoy me looking."

It seemed so self-indulgent, what he was asking of her. Yet, as he touched her, and as his gaze continued to linger upon her, the last of her reticence vanished. When together they had removed all of her clothing, she did not try to hide from him.

"Beautiful," he repeated, his voice husky. "Everything about you is beautiful, Robyn."

She looked at him, too, as his jeans came off, then his underwear. The lines of his body were strong and masculine, stirring her deepest response. She saw the scar left behind by the bullet, and she touched it.

"Does it hurt?" she whispered.

"Nothing hurts right now. Robyn…"

Their limbs tangled together as they lay on the

futon. But Mark refused to rush anything. He caressed her until she thought the longing would burst inside her, and he watched her face as if to savor every bit of her pleasure. And then she knew the secret of what Mark gave her. Instead of hurrying to fulfill his own needs, he took pleasure in her enjoyment. His fingers moved over the soft bare skin of her stomach, trailed below. As he touched her intimately, he gazed straight into her eyes, and he smiled as at last her longing could no longer be contained. She came with one ragged gasp after another.

She was still breathing unsteadily a moment or two later as she guided him inside her. She was amazed that the wanting could build so quickly again, but this time she desired *his* pleasure most of all. Their bodies locked together, their eyes locked, they moved in a powerful rhythm that swept both of them on a crest of sensation. Her cries mingled with his groans, and never once did they look away from each other.

It was only afterward that Robyn tore her gaze from Mark's, only afterward that she turned on her side so that he would not see her face. They ended up in the classic spoon position, her backside tucked against him. She closed her eyes tightly, as if that would make her forget exactly how reckless she'd just been.

One mistake, you could excuse. But two mistakes...for that, there was no excuse.

HANNETT PARK WAS the perfect spot for a children's birthday party. The gnarled old cottonwoods provided ample shade, and there were swings and a slippery slide. A volleyball net had been set up, and a game was in progress. Picnic tables scattered here and there provided a staging area for barbecued hamburgers, potato salad and other treats. Robyn stood beside one of the tables, watching as kids ran boisterously about. From here, she could see a short way across the park to where Josh sat in one of the swings. A little girl sat in the swing next to his, chattering away to him. Yet Josh scarcely seemed to be listening. His head was bent, and he scuffed his feet in the dirt underneath him. Robyn could only imagine what thoughts might be going through his mind. How did you cope when you were nine years old, and your world had been shattered? Even if it wasn't the most stable world to begin with...even if you had the kind of mother who blackmailed people and made you pretend she was your sister...even so, if you lost that world, just how did you survive? The kid needed someone to depend on. He'd need professional counseling too, if he was going to make it through this mess.

Mark had been talking to his friend Benjamin, but

now he came across the park to Robyn. "From all reports, Josh has been quiet and withdrawn all day," he said. "Benjamin persuaded him to join in a softball game, but Josh didn't show a whole lot of enthusiasm. I suspect he's afraid to have any fun—he probably sees that as being disloyal to Emily."

"She may have done some rotten things in her life, but she certainly inspired love," Robyn murmured. "Randall Garrett, her son, perhaps even my father for a time...I wonder who else loved her." She turned away from Mark, even as she spoke.

"Robyn," he said gravely, "you can't keep doing that. Acting as if we didn't make love only a few hours ago—"

"Stop, Mark. Please." Nobody else was near, but that picnic table under the cottonwood provided her an excellent way to busy herself. "I'm going to fix myself a hamburger," she said. "I never did have lunch, what with... I'm hungry, that's all." In reality, her appetite had deserted her, but Mark didn't need to know about that.

She went up to the table, took a paper plate and put a bun on it. Then she picked up the mustard. Mark came and stood beside her.

"I'll be glad to fix you a plate, too," she said, "but maybe you could do something else in the meantime."

He stayed right where he was. "Robyn, I thought

we were going to be honest with each other. Something's bothering you, and I'd like to know what it is."

Robyn put too much mustard onto her bun. "Everything is disintegrating around me—of course I'm bothered."

"I'm talking about you and me," he said.

Now she squirted some catsup on the bun, finished off the job with a grilled hamburger and scattered some potato chips willy-nilly on her plate. She didn't see how she could possibly eat any of this—not with the way her stomach had clenched into a knot.

She sat down at the picnic table, and Mark sat across from her. She tried to nibble on a potato chip, but she might as well have been eating sawdust.

"Okay," she said. "I'll tell you what's wrong. Back at your apartment, before we…before we made love, I told you that I might be starting to feel something more for you. I admitted it, told you how much it scared me. But you, Mark…you talk about honesty, but you've given nothing away. I don't even have a clue how *you* feel."

"Robyn, maybe I'm just like you—trying to sort things out. Trying to figure out where we go from here. But I have a track record that doesn't give me a lot of encouragement."

"Right," she muttered. "You're no good at relationships. And neither am I. So where *do* we go, Mark?''

He didn't have an answer, and she didn't expect one. She pushed away the plate of food she'd prepared. With her family disintegrating and Josh to worry about, the last thing she needed was... confusing new feelings for Mark Stewart that she didn't know what on earth to do with.

"Robyn, there you are!" came a voice behind her. It was the instantly recognizable voice of her mother.

She twisted around. "Mom, what on earth are you doing here?"

Nina looked distraught as she came over the grass. "You said you'd be picking up Josh here. I took a chance I'd find you. There's something you have to know...it's not the type of thing that can wait..."

Robyn made her mother sit down at the picnic table. Mark didn't try to intervene, and Robyn was grateful for that.

"Tell me what it is," she said.

Nina clasped her hands together, but she couldn't disguise the fact that they were shaking. "Where to start," she said, her voice strained. "Your uncle Greg hasn't shown up yet, but your aunt Janet broke down and told me...well, it seems Greg was having an affair with Emily, too."

At this pronouncement, all Robyn could do was turn and look at Mark. He took the news with his usual aplomb, as if nothing in the world could surprise him.

"Was your sister-in-law absolutely certain of this, Mrs. Myers?" he asked.

"She caught the two of them together one day," Nina said. "She'd been suspecting that something was wrong, and when she saw Greg and Emily together..."

Robyn still couldn't take it in. "Uncle Greg...and Emily...where does it end?" Cal Myers, his brother, Greg, Randall Garrett. Just how many men had Emily entranced? But Nina was already going on.

"Janet says she overhead you talking with your father this morning. She was kind enough to fill me in. At least now we know what he did with the money from the savings account." Nina spoke like someone in shock. "And Janet says you and your father also discussed the possibility that he might have murdered Emily. What with her blackmailing him, and all...but now it seems he has another motive for murder, doesn't it?"

"Mom, what are you saying—"

"It's perfectly clear to me. Your father loses his head over a pretty young woman. And then he finds out that the pretty young woman is stepping out with his own brother behind his back. It seems perfectly reasonable that he'd shoot the pretty young woman." Nina's hands were truly shaking now. "That's what I told Detective Garrett, anyway," she said. "I called him on the telephone and told him that it's very likely your father killed Emily. I explained everything about your father's possible motives. I must say, Detective Granger is very efficient. He came right over to the house, but this time it wasn't just to ask more questions. He took your father into custody."

CHAPTER FIFTEEN

LESS THAN AN HOUR LATER, Mark was sitting across from Detective Tom Granger. At Robyn's request, he'd come down to the station to learn what he could about her father's status. "Please, Mark," she'd said urgently. "Just find out what's happening with my dad...please."

So here he was with Tom. This afternoon Tom wore a double-breasted herringbone suit, the kind that might have looked good if you were taking a jaunt at an English country estate. In a Santa Fe police office, it looked overdone.

"You know you don't have enough evidence to arrest Cal Myers," Mark said.

"Stewart, they ever give me any time off from this place, I'm actually going to take it. Unlike you, I know the meaning of the word *vacation*. I'm going to put my feet up, and do some fishing, and not much else."

Mark doubted that Tom Granger had ever been fishing in his life. "You don't have enough on Cal Myers," he repeated. "Not enough to arrest him."

"He's not under arrest," Tom said. "Not yet. We've just brought him in for more questioning. As far as what we do have on the guy, how's motive and opportunity sound? Not only was he doing the deceased, but she was blackmailing him, to boot. Estimated time of death is between 10:00 p.m. and midnight. Nina Myers assumes her husband was sleeping during that time, but she was in another part of the house so she can't be sure. No one else in the family can swear that he stayed put during those two hours. The guy sneaks out of the house, no sweat. He has a broken arm, but it's the left one. He can still drive, he can still pull a trigger."

"All circumstantial, Tom," Mark said, "and you know it. There are other leads to pursue. Randall Garrett, for instance, and any other men in Emily Parkman's life—"

"We have everything under control," Tom said confidently. "Even without you around, we're managing to do our job. We're not leaving any possibility uncovered. That includes Greg Myers—we're looking for him, and we'll bring him in for questioning, too. Now, don't you have a *vacation* to get on with? This isn't your case, Stewart, no matter how pretty the suspect's daughter is. Thought the captain reminded you of that."

Mark could tell he wouldn't get anything else out

of Tom, and he rose to go. He was almost out the door when Tom came up with an addendum.

"Say, speaking of daughters, that daughter of yours has been around a lot, asking questions about the Parkman case. Debra, isn't that her name? She's persistent, I'll give her that."

So Debbie was going ahead, with or without Mark's blessing. He'd expected as much, but it didn't help to hear it. His daughters wouldn't take advice from him...

They wouldn't take anything at all.

SURELY THE SIGN of a true optimist was someone who could find a bright spot in the darkest situation. If so, Robyn knew she'd proven herself a first-class optimist. Yesterday, due to lack of evidence, the police had released her father in the late afternoon. In this whole sorry mess, she seized on that one fact—her father had not been officially accused of Emily's murder. Whatever her private fears about his innocence, at least she had that much.

Now she watched as Josh wandered along the pebbly shore of Cochiti Lake. This was the one place where it seemed Josh wanted to be. Evidently, Emily had brought him here on outings several times. Only a short distance from Santa Fe, Cochiti was a man-made lake that stretched a dazzling blue

under the equally dazzling New Mexico sky. Sail-
boats skimmed the water like white wings.

Mark came up behind Robyn. "This was a good
idea," he said.

"I hope so," she murmured. A few moments ago,
she and Mark had stood at the shore and talked to
Josh about Emily a bit. They'd encouraged him to
speak about her, too. After that, he'd walked quickly
ahead, making it clear that he needed to be alone.
Robyn was keeping an eye on him, but she would
allow him his solitude. That was part of grieving,
after all.

"I wonder if I'll ever understand Emily," she
said, her voice low. "The more I learn about her,
the more upset I get. She's practically destroyed my
family...I mean, did she have to go after my father
and my uncle *both?* For all I know, she was trying
to blackmail Uncle Greg, too. What a way to make
a buck. Maybe that's why she told everyone Josh
was her brother, not her son—maybe it made her
blackmail schemes easier. I really could hate her.
And yet, I look at that kid she produced, and I can't
think she was all bad."

"Nobody's all bad," Mark said.

She glanced at him in surprise. "This is the hardened policeman talking?"

"Maybe I've changed my mind. Maybe I'm not
such a cynic anymore."

She didn't trust his words. She was careful not to look at him right now, focusing only on the deep blue of the lake.

"I wonder how Mom's doing," she said. "I didn't like leaving her today, but Josh's needs seemed more important for the moment. My poor mother, though…she finally found a way to get back at Dad. Practically accusing him of murder, having him hauled in by the police."

Mark didn't answer. He, too, stood gazing at the lake, his profile intent. Robyn had to remind herself not to look at him, not to examine the details about him: his dark wind-brushed hair, the crinkles at the corners of his eyes, the strong line of his jaw…

She swiveled forward again.

"Robyn," Mark said. "We can't avoid talking about us." He took her hand, and they stood there close together at the edge of the lake.

"What do you see for us, Mark?" she asked after a long moment. "I go to your bed again? And then what?"

"I don't know," he said, frowning a little. "I only know that I want you, Robyn. And I'm pretty sure you want me, too. Maybe we'll just have to take it one step at a time."

She moved her fingers inside his grasp. "No, Mark," she said, her voice tight. "We can't take it any further at all. Not while everything's in such confusion around us. And besides, wanting isn't enough. There has to be something more."

He didn't answer. He didn't offer her anything more. And, at last, she slipped her hand away from his.

ON THE WAY BACK to Santa Fe, Mark and Robyn didn't speak to each other for quite some time. Josh lay curled in the back seat. Robyn wanted to say something reassuring, but nothing came to mind. She ended up muttering something under her breath, and Mark glanced at her briefly as he drove.

"Didn't catch that," he said.

"It was nothing." She peered over her shoulder at Josh. "You okay back there?"

"I'm fine." Josh sounded very adult, despite the cowlick and slightly sunburned nose.

Robyn twisted forward again. "You know, Mark," she said as casually as possible, "you do realize that my life may be rather complicated in the future. There's a certain…package I intend to hold on to, if it's at all possible."

She knew he would understand what she meant: if none of Josh's relatives could be found, then Robyn herself would try to keep him somehow. She'd even started to hope that she might be able to adopt Josh. There was something about the little boy that got to her. Maybe it was his loneliness, and the way he tried so hard to be brave in spite of everything that had happened to him. Maybe it was just that behind his proud, withdrawn exterior was a kid who desperately needed a home. And she desperately wanted to provide one.

"Those kinds of packages are a big responsibility," Mark said.

"What's in the package?" Josh asked from the back seat.

Robyn found herself giving an unexpected laugh. "All kinds of good things, Josh. A lot of fun...but I suppose a lot of worry, too. You can't have one without the other."

"Yeah, well, that's kind of how I feel about having a dog," Josh said.

"You want a dog?" Robyn asked.

"Yeah. A Scottie."

"A Scottie dog," Robyn echoed.

"Sounds like a full house to me," Mark said.

A house...she certainly hadn't thought *that* far ahead. But if you were lucky enough to end up with a little boy and a dog, you probably did need a real home. She tried to envision it, but the only house that came to mind was the one out there in the foothills. Green trim, adobe walls...

Robyn gazed out the windshield, wondering if Mark had decided whether or not he was going to buy the house. She kept herself from asking, though.

She was relieved when they drove into Santa Fe and finally arrived at Mark's apartment.

The telephone was ringing as they went in. Mark answered it, then handed the receiver to her.

"It's your father," he said.

Immediately she felt apprehensive. She took the receiver, pressed it to her ear. "Dad—what's up? Are you all right? Where are you?"

"I'm fine, Robyn," came his voice. "But yes, in response to your first question, something's up." Cal sounded more assured than he had in a long while. Somehow, that did nothing to soothe Robyn's foreboding.

"Exactly what *is* up, Dad?"

"Your mother's not speaking to me, and there are a few things I need to tell someone, Robyn, just in case. It's time I was honest with myself. It's time I faced up to the problems I've caused."

She gripped the receiver. "Dad, you're resting, aren't you? You've been through an ordeal with the police, and you should rest—"

"I don't have much time, Robyn, so listen. I'm tired of being afraid...so very tired of it. I won't be that way anymore. Honey, I begged you to get a gun to protect yourself and your mother. You wouldn't do it, and perhaps rightly so. It's up to me to do the protecting."

"Dad—"

"You don't need to worry how. These things are actually quite easy if you have a friend who knows a friend, and so forth. The point is, I have a gun now, and I'm going to meet him. I will no longer let him endanger me or my family."

Robyn held the receiver so tightly that her fingers ached. She looked at Mark, saw the concern on his face, but she had to keep talking to her father. At all costs, that was what she had to do.

"Who are you going to meet, Dad?" she asked as calmly as possible.

"Why, the man who attacked me. The man who is still threatening to harm you and your mother. The man who killed Emily."

"Dad, this is something for the police to handle. Please, Dad—"

"You think the police are going to believe me now, Robyn? They think *I* killed Emily. Besides, I finally need to stand up for myself...and for the people I love. I have to do it on my own, or I'll never be able to live with myself."

"No, Dad—"

"I'm only telling you this in case things don't go well for me. It's a possibility I have to acknowledge. This guy's already killed once. But right now I'm going to meet him...where it all started. I love you, Robyn. Please know that. I love you and your mother very much." The line suddenly went dead.

The receiver fell from Robyn's fingers, but she scarcely noticed. For a second or two she felt a wave of sickness. She saw Mark's face, Josh's face, and they both seemed to waver in front of her.

"Where's your father going, Robyn?" Mark asked. Something about his quiet tone helped to steady her. The nausea passed, and she felt oddly composed.

"Dad has a gun, and some terribly misguided idea about proving his courage. He said he was going to meet the man who killed Emily. He said he would go to where it all started...the art gallery, Mark. That must be what he meant—that's where he was attacked in the first place. We have to get there ourselves, as quickly as possible."

IT SEEMED to Robyn that Mark broke every speed limit in the city. The Land Cruiser, in spite of its age, rose to the occasion. It surged down one street, roared down another. Both Josh and Robyn had to cling to their seats as the vehicle skidded around a corner and accelerated all the more. But time continued to pass nonetheless—the seconds stretched into minutes.

"Please," Robyn murmured over and over. "Please let us get there...before it's too late..."

Mark had already been on the cell phone, requesting backup. The Land Cruiser, however, was the first to career into the parking lot of the gallery. Barely had it jolted to a halt before Robyn scrambled out. She wished there'd been time to leave Josh somewhere else, but there was no time for anything, it seemed. As if in a nightmare, she heard the staccato sounds of two gunshots, one right after the other.

"You and Josh, stay here," Mark commanded, and then he disappeared inside the gallery. Robyn's first instinct was to protect Josh, and she held him close to her side. Only a few seconds later, two police cars screeched into the parking lot. And, meanwhile, scuffling noises came from the gallery.

Robyn could wait no longer. "Stay right here with one of the officers," she told Josh, and then she crept toward the door to look inside the gallery.

Mark had worked with impressive swiftness. Already he had wrestled a man to the floor—a man none other than Randall Garrett. Garrett's features had swollen with rage, but his cheek was pressed into the rug, his arms twisted behind him by Mark.

"I'm not the one you want," rasped Garrett. "Myers killed her—that bastard's the one who did it!"

Cal lay in a heap, his face truly battered this time. His arm was flung out, as if reaching toward the gun on the floor beside him, but he was unconscious. Robyn fell to her knees next to him.

"Dad..." Her voice came on a sob. As if from a great distance, she heard Randall Garrett ranting on.

"She never should have looked at that bastard. What did she need him for? I could have given her everything she wanted...if she'd only given me a chance. I loved her...I didn't kill her. He's the one you want."

Robyn leaned over her father, wishing she could force life into him. She couldn't even tell if he was breathing. And then, even as more sirens wailed in the parking lot outside, Josh knelt beside her and took her hand.

"It'll be okay, Robyn," he said. With another sob, she gathered the little boy close to her, and prayed that her father wouldn't die.

THE OPEN-AIR CAFÉ just off the plaza was Santa Fe's attempt at Parisian atmosphere, with brightly colored awnings and menus in French and a liberal supply of croissants. Mark wondered why Santa Fe needed a dose of Paris when the Southwest was exotic enough on its own. Then again, maybe he needed to stretch his horizons. Maybe he needed to be a little more cosmopolitan.

He sat at one of the outdoor tables and spread the Albuquerque newspaper open in front of him. The article about Emily Parkman's murder didn't show up till the third page, toward the bottom; world and metropolitan news took precedence. But the article carried the byline of Debra Stewart, and it was a well-written account that brought the facts of the case up-to-date. It appeared Debra was going to be a crime reporter—and a good one, at that—no matter what he had to say about it. He read the article for the second time.

It stated that yesterday afternoon, Santa Fe police had arrested real estate agent Randall Garrett for the murder of twenty-six-year-old Emily Parkman. It seemed, the article relayed, that Emily had developed a habit of getting men into compromising situations then blackmailing them. Although it was not clear whether eventually she planned to blackmail Garrett, he had allowed her to stay at some of the houses his agency listed for sale. When Garrett had discovered Emily's affair with Cal Myers, a local art gallery owner, Garrett had not only attacked Myers, but threatened to harm Myers's family. Apparently, Garrett had not been able to tolerate the thought of Emily with anyone but himself, and police speculated that this was his motive for killing her. Even after her death, Garrett had attacked Cal Myers a second time. And now Myers lay unconscious in a Santa Fe hospital room.

Mark could have filled in a few other details. Randall Garrett claimed that he was not the murderer. Instead, he accused Robyn's father of the crime. Yesterday, the two men had confronted each other at the art gallery, and Cal had attempted to defend himself. His gun had gone off twice. The bullets hadn't hit anyone, but Garrett had beaten up Cal in a rage and this time nearly killed him. Doctors could not say whether Cal Myers would survive.

Mark set down the newspaper. At this moment, Robyn was with her father in the hospital, refusing to leave his side. Mark had seen to some necessary arrangements, such as having Josh stay with Benjamin. Then Mark had spent as much time as possible with Robyn. Only one thing could have pulled him away from her...the one thing he had to do today.

He glanced up and saw his two daughters approaching him along the sidewalk. When they reached his table, they both surveyed him distrustfully.

"What's this all about, Father?" Debra asked.

"What could be so important that you had us drive up from Albuquerque?" Kerry added.

"Please...have a seat," he told them. "It is important—very, very important."

He waited until each of them had sat down reluctantly. Then he reached into the pocket of his jacket and took out some folded sheets of paper. They were somewhat crinkled with age, but he smoothed them on the table.

"I've never shown this to either of you girls, but these are the terms of the divorce agreement with your mother," he said. "Custody stipulations. The way things are set out, I get you girls every other weekend and one month during the summer. Those were and *are* my legal rights as your parent."

His daughters looked at him with varying degrees of disbelief.

"But, Father," Debra said, "we're not children anymore. We're adults."

"Is he feeling okay?" Kerry asked. "Maybe he's been drinking."

"No, I haven't been drinking," Mark said. "And I'm feeling fine. Here's how it is. In the past, none of us has abided by this custody agreement. Either I'd have a case I couldn't get away from, or the two of you would have an excuse why you couldn't be with me. That's about to change. I'm here—I'm a fact of your lives. No more excuses from any of us. You're my daughters…I'm your father. No—I'm your dad. And there's nothing you can do about it."

Both daughters stared at him in amazement. Neither seemed able to speak.

"I'm sorry," Mark continued. "I'm sorry I wasn't there for you. But I'm here now and I'm not going away. Thinking back, I realize there's something I haven't told you girls for a long time, either one of you. I love you. I love you both." He smoothed out the crinkled sheets of paper again, but he couldn't seem to focus on the print. "Every other weekend," he said. "One month in the summer. It was my legal right then, and I neglected it. But now, I want to be your dad."

Kerry and Debra looked at each other. Debra's face remained hard. But then, unexpectedly, Kerry burst into tears.

"I've been so unhappy," she said shakily. "I just haven't been thinking straight. I was so scared to get married, and I blamed you, and I blamed Frederick. But you know what he told me last night? He told me the only reason he's been so distracted lately is because's he's worried he won't get a job. And even *after* he told me that, I shut the door in his face! Am I a jerk, or what?"

"You're not a jerk," Mark said. "You're a wonderful girl who's had a lousy father. No wonder you're scared to get married."

"You tried to help. You tried to tell me Frederick wasn't such a bad guy. Oh…Dad!" Kerry erupted in tears again. And then she scooted her chair next to his and flung herself into his arms.

It had been so long since he'd held one of his daughters that he didn't know what to do at first. He patted Kerry's back awkwardly. He didn't care about the people looking over in unfeigned curiosity. He didn't care about anything except that one of his kids had just called him "Dad." Not Father...*Dad.*

"About those custody arrangements," he said. "I'm holding you to them, you know."

Kerry sobbed all the harder. Mark went on holding his youngest daughter, but his older daughter remained seated rigidly where she was. The expression on her face said it all: maybe her kid sister was swayed by all this, but not *her.*

Debra wasn't buying.

CHAPTER SIXTEEN

ROBYN SAT BESIDE her father's bed in the dim hospital room. A nurse had come in earlier to draw the shades, and now the afternoon sun barely trickled in. Robyn was grateful. It was better this way, her father's face cast in shadow. She could pretend that he was only sleeping, and not unconscious.

Her throat was raw from talking to him. She'd felt foolish at first. She'd watched enough of those coma scenes on television and at the movies, where people gathered at the bedside and said all manner of things to their unconscious loved ones. But now, for the first time, she understood the scenario. You had to talk, and you had to believe that somehow the talking would get through. Otherwise, you might entirely lose hope. Robyn couldn't face that—she couldn't lose hope.

And so she talked to her father. She was as honest and straightforward as she could be, too. When he'd made the telephone call to her yesterday, he'd stated that he no longer wanted to hide from his fears. And that meant he didn't want to hide from the truth. Robyn hoped he meant what he'd said.

"Mom has been at your bedside constantly," Robyn said now. "The only reason she's not here right this minute is that I insisted she go get something to eat. She's still so devoted to you, Dad—but that doesn't change the fact that she's still angry, too. You really hurt her, I'm afraid. And you'll hurt all of us even more if you don't come back to us."

She took hold of her father's hand, and chafed it between her own. "*I'm* still ticked at you, Dad," she said. "I wish you'd wake up so I could tell you just how mad I am. The first time Randall Garrett attacked you, that's when you should have told the police about him—regardless of his threats. As for yesterday, I know you thought you had to stand up for yourself and your family, and that's why you went off to meet Garrett. But why did you have to do it on your own? Did you think it was the only way to redeem yourself? Couldn't you have found another way to prove your courage?"

His hand remained limp and lifeless in hers. She had to strain to hear the sound of his breathing. "Please wake up, Dad," she begged. "Please…"

"Your dad will make it, honey," Uncle Greg said as he stepped into the room. "You have to believe that."

"Oh, Uncle Greg, you're back! Thank goodness." Robyn stood, and began going toward him.

"When you know everything, Robyn," he said quietly, "you won't wish I was back."

Something in his tone made her stop. His expression was all too familiar. It carried the bleakness she'd observed in her father's eyes.

"I already know about you and Emily," she said. "It's out in the open, Uncle Greg. But right now, all I want is my family around me again."

"It's what I want, too," Greg said. "But it's too late…far too late."

Her father had uttered those words, too. Robyn watched as her uncle sat down next to the hospital bed. He didn't seem quite so big and solid as he always had. His face was too pale.

"Uncle Greg, we were all so worried about you. Your heart, for one thing…"

"These past few days, my health has been the least of my worries. I've been up in the Jémez by myself, doing a lot of soul-searching. And I can only blame myself for everything that's happened."

Childhood memories came to Robyn: family camping trips in the Jémez Mountains, times when she'd been surrounded by the love of her parents, her aunt and uncle.

"Robyn, what I'm going to say isn't easy, but I'd just better get on with it. You're the one to hear it—you're the one who'll carry on this family, or what's left of it.''

Robyn stood where she was, arms held tightly against her body, dreading what he would tell her.

''Your aunt and I…we both wanted children so very much, Robyn. We had all the tests, did everything we could. Yet still it didn't happen. Finally we began to think of adoption, but that wasn't the solution for Janet. She felt that giving birth to a child was the only way she could prove herself as a woman. That idea had been so ingrained in her by her own parents, nothing I said seemed to reassure her. And gradually, Robyn, we began to grow apart.''

''To me, you always seemed so happy,'' she murmured.

''On the surface, yes, I suppose we did appear to be getting along. But underneath…Janet kept accusing herself for what she saw as her failure. She wouldn't allow it to be a burden that belonged to both of us. Because she couldn't be a mother herself, she mothered every sick and wounded creature she found. But when it came to our marriage, over the years she just kept withdrawing more and more. No matter what I said or did, she seemed convinced *I* saw her as a failure.''

''Oh, Uncle Greg, I never realized—''

''It wasn't something either one of us knew how

to share. But I finally realized we couldn't go on like that. I moved out. I felt anything was better than all the silences between us. Then I had the heart attack—and we were both shook up at the idea I could have died. It brought us closer for a time. I moved back in, hoping...but eventually the old patterns returned. Janet started withdrawing again. I didn't know what to do next, where to turn. Then your mother hired Emily Parkman to work in the gift shop. It had been a long time since any woman had looked at me the way Emily did. I even forgot I had a heart condition. I just felt alive—and wanted." Greg paused. "Robyn, I'm not telling you any of this to take myself off the hook. Janet and I were having problems, but that didn't mean I had to have an affair. The damn affair that set everything else in motion."

After that, Greg didn't speak for a few moments. Robyn sensed, however, that the worst was to come. At last he leaned forward, wearily resting his elbows on his knees.

"Janet could tell something was going on, and she started following me. She found Emily and me together. The details don't matter—they were sordid enough. But I'll never forget the look of hurt on Janet's face. I realized then that she had never stopped loving me—and I'd repaid her with the worst kind of betrayal. I could see how it must have seemed through her eyes—I'd made love to a young, beautiful woman...one who could, no doubt, bear children. Nothing could have made Janet feel more like a failure. Being the cause of that terrible hurt—I won't forgive myself for that, Robyn. Never.''

Robyn sat down on the other side of the hospital bed. She gazed at her father...still unconscious. She didn't excuse either her father or her uncle for what they'd done, but she loved them nonetheless. Her feelings toward Emily Parkman were somewhat different. Now, for the first time, she genuinely hated the woman for all the destruction she had wrought.

"Uncle Greg, did Emily ever try to blackmail you?"

"No, but after everything I've learned about her, I believe that was what she intended. She knew I'd do anything not to have Janet find out, but Janet walked in on us, and that must have changed Emily's plans. I broke off the affair right away, but of course it was too late. Janet's trust in me was destroyed, and she refused to believe I'd stopped seeing Emily. Robyn, do you remember the night at the art gallery, when someone came in and disturbed you?"

"Of course I do." The door, swinging wide to darkness...

"I'd gone out for a drive that night, just trying to think my way through the mess I'd made. Janet came after me, but she lost sight of my car. She did see the lights on in the gallery, and thought perhaps I was there—with Emily. She crept inside, but when she realized it was you and your friend Mark, she retreated as fast as she could. But I didn't learn all this until…until the night Janet killed Emily.'' His voice seemed to have gone hollow.

Robyn sat frozen in her chair. "No! You have to be wrong. The real estate agent Randall Garrett killed Emily. Aunt Janet would never hurt anyone."

He bowed his head. "Afterward she told me that she didn't mean to do it. She only bought a gun for protection. After the attack on Cal, she was scared. She'd overheard your father pressuring *you* to get a gun, and she decided to get one herself. Then, after she learned Emily and I were having an affair, she thought she'd use the gun for different purposes. She asked Emily to meet her at the gift shop. She showed the gun, brandished it a little, and that was supposed to be all. It was supposed to convince Emily to leave me alone. Except then, according to Janet, Emily gave her a look of such contemptuous pity…and Emily said no man would want a defective wife…an infertile wife. She knew the most cruel thing to say because I had confided our problems to her. I believe Janet saw that as the worst betrayal of all…and then she pulled the trigger."

"No," Robyn whispered. "Please, no…"

"Janet was hysterical afterward, and she told me everything. But then I made the wrong choice, Robyn. I should have taken her to the police. Having Janet confess right then would have helped her case. But I couldn't do it...I couldn't bear to turn in my wife to the authorities. Rather than do that, I left for the Jémez Mountains. I had to be by myself, had to try sorting everything out on my own. Then I went down for supplies, and I saw the story about my brother in the newspapers. I read about this man Randall Garrett, and how he'd been the one to attack Cal. I realized if Garrett had known about *my* involvement, he would have come after me, too. But I don't feel lucky to have escaped, Robyn. I just wish it was me in this hospital bed, not my brother. And now I have to do the right thing for all of us. Even if it *is* too late, I'll try to make the police see that Janet's not truly to blame..."

Just then Janet herself came into the hospital room. Her face was streaked with tears.

"Greg..." Her voice wavered. "I heard everything you said. I've been standing outside, listening. I'm getting altogether too good at that, listening outside doors."

He stood and walked toward her. She reached inside her purse, pulled out a gun. Greg stopped.

Janet gave him a stricken look. "I'm not going to shoot. It's not even loaded. I just wanted to show you I had the same idea as you…I meant to turn myself in. I brought this along…the murder weapon…so the police would have everything they need." She gazed at the gun in her hand with a kind of horror, then swiveled toward the hospital bed. "But first I need to ask my brother-in-law to forgive me. Even though he can't hear me, I have to say it." Her voice trembled all the more. "Cal, I'm so sorry I let everyone think you were guilty. I was terrified after it happened…after I did it. And so I let them blame you. I'm so terribly sorry. If I'd confessed right away, you probably wouldn't be here…" The gun dropped from Janet's fingers, skittering across the floor, and she seemed about to crumple. It was Uncle Greg who caught her, held her close.

"Somehow it will be all right, love," he told her. "Somehow we'll make it all right. And I'll never leave you again, not ever. Hush, now. I'll never leave you…"

ROBYN STOOD under one of the cottonwoods at Hannett Park. The spring breeze drifted over her, as if attempting to warm the chill deep in her bones. She wondered if anything could ever warm her again. Mark stood beside her.

"How are you doing?" he asked quietly.

"I'll make it…I suppose." She gazed across the

park to where nine-year-old Josh sat on a picnic bench, flanked by a man and woman. Both the man and woman leaned toward the little boy as if they could not get enough of him…as if they marveled at his very existence. And well they should. They were Josh's grandparents, and until yesterday they hadn't even known of his existence.

After tracing through the complexities of Emily Parkman's life, the police had finally located her parents alive and well—Daniel and Luisa, residents of San Francisco, California. Upon being contacted, they had immediately flown to Albuquerque, and from there rented a car that would bring them to Santa Fe. Robyn had asked only that she be allowed to hand Josh over to them. She'd chosen to do so in the park because it was the kind of place you could imagine families getting off to a good start.

From what she could see at this distance, Josh was taking the measure of both his grandparents. It was difficult to tell if he'd decided on a verdict yet, but at least he was sitting there in dignified fashion, letting the two of them get acquainted with him.

Mark put his arm around Robyn and held her close to his side. "Whatever you need to do right now is okay," he said.

"Mark, I'm not going to lose control and do something horrible or embarrassing. Even though what I really feel like doing is snatching up Josh and running away with him as fast as I can..." She felt her voice catch, and she had to wait a few seconds before she went on. "They seem like nice people, don't they?"

"From what I've seen—yes."

"Bewildered people," Robyn said. "I can't imagine what it would be like to have your daughter run away from home at sixteen. Not to have any clue where she's gone, and to look for her all those years...and then to find out she's been killed, and left a little boy behind." She took a deep breath, but it did nothing to steady her. "Do you think Josh's father will ever be found?"

"I doubt it," Mark said. "There aren't any traces so far."

From Robyn's vantage point, she stared hard at Emily's parents. "Dammit, Mark," she said fiercely. "They'd *better* be nice people. They'd better not be the ones who made Emily so jaded and conniving!"

Mark's arm tightened around her. "The authorities both here and in California will make certain they can provide Josh with a good home. But they're his family, Robyn—they have to be given a chance."

She knew what he was saying was true, but it didn't change one fact. She'd been hoping all along that *she* would be Josh's family.

Josh's grandmother stood and came toward Robyn. She was a pretty woman, with features very like Emily's. Tears shimmered in her eyes, but she blinked to keep them from falling. That was like Josh. "Ms. Myers," she said, "could I talk to you for a moment?"

Robyn nodded, not trusting herself to speak. Mark stepped away.

"I'll be nearby if you need me," he said.

"I'll be fine," she managed to say. Josh's grandmother blotted her eyes with a handkerchief, and then she gave Robyn a thoughtful look.

"Ms. Myers, I can tell that you care about Josh."

"Please, call me Robyn. And yes...I do care. He's special."

Luisa smiled softly. "Yes, he is special, isn't he? Ms. Myers—Robyn. I know that my daughter did some terrible things. I understand that she hurt your family, and for that I am very sorry. But I want you to know...I don't believe Emily was a bad person, not at heart. When she was a teenager, she fell in with the wrong kind of people, that's all. We tried to stop her. We tried to help—but then she left us. We were so worried about her, and then so angry. And then we were just afraid that maybe she felt too ashamed to come home. Afraid that maybe she had traveled too far from us. If only she had known...all we wanted was for her to come home."

On impulse, Robyn reached out and took the older woman's hand. "I'm sure Emily thought about you a lot. And somehow I'm sure that she did want to go home. Perhaps she just didn't know how to find her way. And she loved Josh. I could see it every time she looked at him."

"Thank you, Robyn." Luisa gave her a tremulous smile.

Now Daniel, Josh's grandfather, came across the grass, walking hand in hand with Josh. He was a rumpled-looking man with a kindly face. Although his hair was turning gray, there were still hints of light brown here and there, almost the same tawny shade as Josh's cowlick. Right now Daniel had an aura of mingled sadness and joy. He, too, gave Robyn a heartfelt smile.

"Thank you," he said simply.

Robyn realized she had already started to trust both these people. She knew instinctively that they would do their best for Josh. Now she knelt beside the boy.

"Josh," she said, amazed that her voice wasn't shaking. "You're going to enjoy San Francisco, you know. It's a great town."

"Have you been there?" he asked.

"Yes. And I had the most wonderful time. The trolley cars, the wharves...trust me, you're in for a treat."

"Will you come to visit, Robyn?"

"Of course she will," Luisa said. "She has a standing invitation. San Francisco isn't so far, not by plane."

"Of course I'll come," Robyn echoed. "We're friends now, aren't we? I'm not just your tutor anymore, am I?"

Josh nodded.

"You'll give school a chance, won't you?" she asked.

"Maybe."

"For Emily," she said. "For your mom."

"Okay." And then he put his arms around her and gave her a surprisingly strong hug. Still holding on to him, and smoothing that stubborn tuft of hair, Robyn spoke to his grandparents.

"Did he tell you he wants a Scottie dog?"

"We told him it's fine," Daniel said, "as long as we start out with a puppy."

"That's the best way to start." Robyn tightened her arms around Josh one last time, and then she let him go. She watched as he shook hands with Mark, man to man. After that, Josh climbed into the rental car. His grandparents climbed in, too. Both Josh and Luisa waved as the car pulled away. And then they were gone.

Robyn hadn't realized she was waiting until now to break down. But almost instantly the tears began to trickle from her eyes, and she thought the ache inside her would sharpen into a pain she couldn't bear. Mark was beside her in just a step or two, his arms engulfing her. She wept into his shirt.

"Oh, Mark, you tried to warn me. You tried to tell me that I should be prepared to give him up."

"You did the right thing," he said, smoothing his fingers over her wet cheek. "You cared about him and that kid needs all the caring he can get."

"I can tell they'll give it to him. But even so, it will take a very long while for him to get over what's happened. And maybe he'll never get over it."

"Emily will always be his mother. His grandparents will make sure he knows that, and it will be the best healing he can have."

She cried all the harder, and Mark patted her back.

"I'm getting good at this," he said. "Having females cry in my arms, and all." He fished in his pocket and produced a handkerchief for her. "This time I'm prepared."

She buried her face in the handkerchief. "Your daughters...?" she asked soggily. "They're the crying females?"

"Only one of them. Kerry's forgiven me. Debra hasn't." His words revealed little, but by now Robyn realized how much he cared about his daughters, how much he needed both of them. She cried harder.

He walked her over to a picnic bench and sat her down. He didn't stop holding her, though, and after a moment he kissed the tears from her cheeks. She turned her mouth to his, and he kissed her for a very long moment, and at last the tears stopped.

Afterward she rested her head against his shoulder. "I don't know what's going to happen," she said. "Mark, what if my father never wakes up? What will I do?"

"No matter what happens, you'll come through. You'll do it for your family. The way you came through for Josh."

"My family…how I wish I could make everything go back the way it used to be. But it was never really as perfect as I thought. Uncle Greg and Aunt Janet were going through so much I never realized. Now, to know Janet will stand trial for murder…how can I bear that, along with everything else? She was so very wrong to do what she did— but she's the aunt who's cared for me almost as much as my own parents…"

Mark's arms tightened around her. "Robyn, I want you to come back to my apartment with me. I want you to stay with me."

If she did that, she knew they would make love again. Robyn would lose herself in his embrace, his caress, and for a few exquisite moments forget everything that had happened. But it would only be a temporary escape.

Slowly she withdrew herself from Mark's arms. Then she stood before him.

"It's not going to work, Mark," she said, struggling against the fresh heartache she felt. "You and I...we really met under the wrong circumstances. I've made the same mistake all over again—getting involved with a man when I'm at my most vulnerable. My career's in chaos, and my family—" Her voice caught. "My family's in tatters, and I can't think about anything else. And you...well, you haven't spoken of love, have you? And neither have I."

"Robyn," he said, "just come home with me."

"You don't have a real home, Mark," she said softly. "Maybe that's where you need to start...a home for yourself."

"I want to be with you, Robyn. And I know you want to be with me—"

"I told you before. Wanting isn't enough."

CHAPTER SEVENTEEN

TODAY THE SHADES in Cal's hospital room were opened wide. Nina insisted that her husband needed sunlight, and plenty of it. No matter that he had been unconscious for almost a week now. She'd arranged everything just as she thought he might like it. She'd brought a coverlet from home to place over his bed, and every day she arranged fresh flowers on the windowsill. This morning she'd also brought in a small painting. Robyn recognized the painting right off. It was one Cal himself had done, and it depicted a sunset over a New Mexico mesa. He'd managed to capture a mood of lonely grandeur. There was nothing bland about Cal's work. It was always bold, evocative.

Nina had propped the painting in a chair beside the bed, and now she sat down in another chair. She spoke to her husband as if he could hear every word she said.

"Things are changing. You and I have pigeon-holed each other too much over the years. I'm supposed to be the one who has a head for business, you're supposed to be the one with all the artistic vision. But, like I say…things are changing. When you see the gallery again, you're going to be in for quite a surprise. I'm right in the middle of arranging an exhibit of Cal Myers's art. Oh, I know you're going to bluster about it, and say you've never wanted anyone to see your paintings. I know your work always falls short in your own eyes. You've always had such impossibly high standards of perfection for your paintings, and when you can't meet them, you despair and shut the door. Well, Cal…I'm opening doors.''

Robyn listened to her mother with a sense of wonder. Nina Myers had found new strength from all of this. Perhaps new lines of grief and strain would be etched permanently into her features now, but she was more forceful, more determined. She leaned close to her husband, clasping his hand as if by her power alone she would will him back to wakefulness.

''We have a lot to talk about, Cal. A great deal, in fact. We have to figure out what brought us to such a point in our lives. You broke trust with me…and it's going to take you a great deal of effort to win my trust back. After that, we'll have to figure out how both of us have been to blame. Did we start taking each other for granted? Did we stop putting enough effort into our marriage? We have to answer the questions, Cal.''

He slept on. Nina leaned closer to him.

"Damn you, Cal Myers…you'd better come back to me. Because after we get through all the difficult stuff, we're finally going on that dream trip of ours. England, Spain…just the two of us. And we're going to rediscover whatever it is we lost along the way…"

Robyn went to place her hands on her mother's shoulders. "You need a break, Mom. I'll sit with him."

Nina stood, but she didn't leave the room. She seemed in a fighting mood. "What about you, Robyn?" she demanded. "What about your own life? Have you finally made a decision about your career?"

"Mom, you don't have to worry about any of that right now—"

"Yes, I do. I've watched this family suffer enough. It's time we started seeing a little hope for the future. And you, Robyn, you're our future.''

Robyn hesitated. "Well, as a matter of fact, I have made a decision. I'm going to teach again, but I'm thinking about doing it a little differently this time. I want to be a tutor—I want to work with kids one-on-one. That's what I discovered with Josh. He made me see that there are kids out there who need me. They don't necessarily have to be my own. Even if I never have children, I can still make a difference.''

"You'll tutor kids, and someday you'll have your own children, too. You'll do all of it and manage quite well, I imagine. Now, what about this Mark Stewart of yours?''

Robyn turned away from her mother. "We don't need to discuss that—''

"You do love him, don't you?''

Robyn went to the window and stared out at the brilliant blue sky. "I think so. But how can I be certain? I'm always falling for men when things are bad in my life, always making wrong decisions about love. Who's to say this time is any different? Besides, I can't possibly think about Mark when Dad's lying in that bed, and Aunt Janet is facing a trial—''

"This is exactly the time to think about love,'' Nina instructed. "Robyn, what your family needs from you *is* hope for the future. And if your future lies with Mark Stewart—grab hold of it. He's not your first husband. He's not even your second husband. But maybe he's a whole new chance at happiness.''

"He says he's lousy at relationships,'' Robyn murmured.

"So maybe it's up to you to convince him otherwise. Robyn, I'd be the last person to tell you there are any guarantees. The older generation in the Myers family has done it wrong in just about every way possible. We allowed Emily Parkman to come into our midst and almost destroy us. We allowed her to find our weaknesses. And yet…I don't think she *has* totally destroyed us. Do you know how much I still love your father? Even Greg and Janet are clinging together in spite of the dreadful uncertainty ahead of them."

What Nina said was true. Robyn had seen it herself: love enduring in her family despite everything.

"Robyn, there are no guarantees," Nina repeated. "But you have to grab hold of your *own* future before it's too late. And that just might mean giving Mark a call."

Robyn sank into the chair beside the hospital bed and put her head down on the coverlet. "I don't know, Mom. I just don't know. Mark hasn't said he loves me. If I call him and he still can't say it…"

She felt a reassuring pat on her head. It was just like when she was a kid, and one of her parents consoled her over a skinned knee or bruised ego. "Thank you, Mom, but I'm not a child anymore," she said. "Life's a whole lot more complicated now."

"Oh, my God," Nina said, and it sounded like a prayer. Only now did Robyn realize that her mother hadn't walked over to pat her head. The one doing the patting was her father.

Robyn nearly jumped out of her chair, and leaned over him. "Dad? Are you back?"

His eyelids fluttered, and opened. He gazed up at Robyn.

"Yes," she whispered. "Dear Lord, you're back."

With an effort, he turned his head and now he gazed at his wife. Nina clasped his hand in her own.

"You weren't getting away from me so easily, dear heart. I'm so furious at you, Cal...but you are my dear heart."

He almost managed a smile. The man and woman who had been married some forty years looked at each other, and in their silence made a new beginning. Robyn watched them for a moment, and then she slipped out of the room.

MARK HAD ALWAYS believed his daughter Kerry to be a lovely girl, but today she'd outdone herself. She was a vision in all that white tulle and lace, a veil floating down over her hair like a mist.

"I'm so nervous," she said as they stood together in the vestibule of the church. "How do I look, Dad? I mean, how do I *really* look?"

"So gorgeous Frederick is probably going to take one look at you and faint right there at the altar."

"He'd better not. He almost fainted already, when he found out he got that job at the software company. They like him, Dad—they say he has great potential. Isn't it wonderful how everything is working out?"

He thought it was wonderful how his youngest daughter kept finding excuses to call him Dad. He just wished his older daughter could find an excuse for it, too. He felt an emptiness whenever he thought about Debra.

Now the organ music was swelling with the "Wedding March." The flower girls had begun their trek down the aisle, and next went the bridesmaids, among them a gorgeous Debra who kept her face turned determinedly away from Mark. In a few seconds it would be Kerry's turn to start down the aisle. She twitched at her veil, bit her lip, and then glanced at him again.

"Give Debra a chance," she said in a low voice.

"I just wish she'd give me a chance," Mark said, his own voice somber.

"She's prickly and difficult—she always has been. But deep down she loves you, Dad." Kerry was trying so hard to make things right. But this was her big day. She deserved to be thinking about other things—such as the groom waiting for her.

"All I know is that I'm going to walk you down that aisle," he said. "Everyone will wonder how I got so lucky to have such a beautiful daughter on my arm. And I am lucky, Kerry. You didn't have to do it, you know. You have a perfectly good step-father—''

"Yes, and a perfectly good father. And fathers are the ones who walk their daughters down the aisle and give them away." She linked her arm in his. "Are you ready?"

"As ready as I'll ever be."

She took a step forward, then paused. "I love you, Dad."

Now they went down the aisle, Kerry seeming to float along on his arm. She gazed ahead at Frederick the entire time. Frederick, the poor guy, *did* look as if he was about to faint. But he also looked as if he'd never seen a vision as stunning as Mark's daughter. In spite of the gangliness of Frederick's limbs, and in spite of the fact that he was definitely too young to be a husband, he did have potential. His new employers were right about that.

Mark's gaze, however, strayed over the guests seated in the church. He was searching for one particular guest...a woman with russet hair and hazel eyes. He'd made certain to have the invitation delivered to her in plenty of time, but he didn't catch a glimpse of her anywhere.

He couldn't keep looking for Robyn, because now he and Kerry had reached the altar. Mark formally gave his daughter away to the waiting groom then stepped back. He was aware of his ex-wife sitting in the front pew, and her husband, Len, sitting beside her. Mark would never be buddies with Len, but he also knew the man *had* been a good stepfather. He was grateful for that.

"We are gathered to witness a pledge between two young people who love each other..." The ceremony proceeded all too quickly. Before Mark knew it, Frederick was kissing Kerry—and his daughter was now a wife.

The reception took place immediately afterward in the grand hall of the church. The place had been festooned with white streamers and countless balloons, and a rock band tuned up on the stage. Eventually Mark got a chance to waltz with the bride, but after that, Frederick monopolized her attention. Mark found himself scanning the hall over and over, looking for that russet-haired woman. She simply did not appear, and he felt a sharp disappointment. Maybe it was too late for them. Maybe they really had met under the wrong circumstances, and nothing could set it right.

Debra walked over. She seemed as remote and cool and self-possessed as always. He wondered if he'd ever find a way to reach his oldest daughter. He wanted to tell her that he loved her, that he'd always be there for her no matter how many mistakes he'd made in the past. But he'd already told her that, and she hadn't listened.

"Where's Trevor?" he asked instead, trying to be casual about the question.

"Trevor and I are no more," she said too lightly. "I gave him an ultimatum, remember? Either get serious, or walk. He walked."

Mark saw the pain in his daughter's eyes, and didn't know how to erase it. "I'm sorry, honey," he said.

"No need to be." She looked away.

"Debbie..."

"Are you going to tell me I'm too good for him?" she asked in a mocking tone.

"You're way too good for him," Mark said. "He doesn't deserve you."

"Oh, Dad—just save it, will you?"

It took him a few seconds to realize what had happened. "You called me Dad," he said. "Maybe it was just a slip of the tongue, but still—"

"Don't overreact. It's not that big of a deal... Dad." Her expression warned him not to get all sentimental. But it *hadn't* been a slip of the tongue. She'd just made that very clear.

With an effort, he remained casual. "According to the custody arrangements, next weekend's mine."

"Kerry will be on her honeymoon, for goodness' sake—"

"I'll pick you up at nine, Debbie."

She looked disgusted, as if she couldn't believe he was subjecting her to such an absurd ritual. But then she gave the briefest of nods, just before one of the groomsmen came to whirl her off into a waltz.

Mark remained where he was. He knew he had a long way to go with Debra. But they'd made a start, and that was all he asked. He searched the crowd again. And there she was, standing just inside the door. Robyn…

He went to her, took her hand, drew her into the center of the floor. Without a word they moved to the music.

"I almost didn't come," Robyn said, curling her hand inside his.

"I was waiting for you. And if you hadn't come, I would have gone after you."

She didn't seem persuaded. "How have you been these past few weeks, Mark?"

He wanted to tell her how much he'd missed her, but he knew he had to proceed carefully.

"I've been putting in time down at the shooting range," he said. "But in another week I'll be back with the department—back on the job."

"Congratulations. I know how much it means to you." Her voice was intentionally neutral.

"Being a detective still means a lot to me, Robyn.

But it's not everything anymore. That's the difference."

She didn't seem to have anything to say to that. She'd consented to dance with him, but maybe she wouldn't consent to much else.

"How have you been?" he asked.

"I'm sure you're aware of the details. My father's slowly on the mend...my uncle has hired the best lawyer possible for my aunt, but of course she'll end up paying for what she did, one way or the other...my family is trying to hold together as best it can."

"And you, Robyn?"

"I'm holding together, too."

Maybe there wasn't any right way to go about this. Maybe he just had to say it. "I love you, Robyn."

She stiffened in his arms. "Mark—"

"Just hear me out," he murmured. He thought he was going to give her a list of arguments, all the reasons he felt the way he did. But then he realized there was only one thing to say. "I love you," he repeated. "I love you more than I thought possible. I'm just a fool for taking so long to figure it out."

She gazed at him with a frown. "Are you saying this because you think it's what I want to hear?"

"I'm saying it because it's true," he said, drawing her close.

She still didn't seem convinced. "What happened to being lousy at relationships?"

"I always thought I was. But now both of my daughters are calling me Dad, and I figure maybe I have more people skills than I realized."

"People skills," she muttered. "Oh, damn. Mark, I love you, too! But it scares the hell out of me. What if I'm just leaning on you because—"

"What if we lean on each other? What if we both have a lot to learn about relationships, and we learn together? What if we face *all* the 'what ifs' together, Robyn..."

She gazed at him for another long moment, and then her breath came on a sigh. "Mark...heaven help me, but I do love you. Turns out I love you to distraction..."

He didn't allow her to say anything more. Instead, he drew her even closer and kissed her as the music played.

"There's only one thing I have to know," he murmured afterward against her cheek.

"Oh...what's that?" She sounded breathless, as if kissing him had taken all of her attention.

"Robyn, how do you feel about a mortgage?"

"It depends," she answered seriously. "Is it for a house in the foothills, a house with green trim?"

"Yes, green trim," Mark repeated. "And adobe walls, and a great view of the mountains."

"Oh, Mark..." Now she was the one who brought him close, her arms holding him fiercely.

He found himself smiling. It felt good. "Robyn, I'm asking you to be my wife."

She started to smile, too. "They say three's a charm. And this time I'm sure I've finally got the right husband. Yes, Mark...I'll marry you. And we can start building that future my mother's always talking about."

The music enveloped them in their own private world. "Just as long as we start with the two of us, we'll be fine," he said.

"The two of us," she repeated. "I like the sound of it. But now...could you say it again?"

He knew what she was asking. He pressed his cheek to hers, and whispered it in her ear. "I love you, Robyn Stewart. I love you with all my heart."

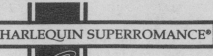

HARLEQUIN SUPERROMANCE®

**Every now and then comes a book that
defies convention, breaks the rules and
still offers the reader all the excitement of
romance. Harlequin Superromance—a series
known for its innovation and variety—
is proud to add these books to our
already outstanding lineup.**

There's more to the story...

RELUCTANT WITNESS (#785)
by Linda Markowiak

Attorney Brent McCade is used to dealing with *hostile*
witnesses. What he can't understand is Sarah Yoder's
reluctance to help him put away the man who has the power
to hurt her again.

Available in April 1998 wherever Harlequin books are sold.

DEBBIE MACOMBER

invites you to the

HEART OF TEXAS

Join Debbie Macomber as she brings you the lives and loves of the folks in the ranching community of Promise, Texas.

If you loved Midnight Sons—don't miss Heart of Texas! A brand-new six-book series from Debbie Macomber.

Available in February 1998 at your favorite retail store.

Heart of Texas by Debbie Macomber

Lonesome Cowboy	February '98
Texas Two-Step	March '98
Caroline's Child	April '98
Dr. Texas	May '98
Nell's Cowboy	June '98
Lone Star Baby	July '98

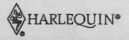

HARLEQUIN®

HPHRT1

Welcome to *Love Inspired*™

A brand-new series of contemporary inspirational love stories.

Join men and women as they learn valuable lessons about facing the challenges of today's world and about life, love and faith.

Look for the following March 1998
Love Inspired™ titles:

CHILD OF HER HEART
by Irene Brand

A FATHER'S LOVE
by Cheryl Wolverton

WITH BABY IN MIND
by Arlene James

Available in retail outlets in February 1998.

LIFT YOUR SPIRITS AND GLADDEN YOUR HEART
with *Love Inspired!*™

Steeple
Hill™

LI398

Don't miss these Harlequin favorites by some of our top-selling authors!